# Freak City

by Tom Lichtenberg

copyright 2009 by Tom Lichtenberg
ISBN: 978-0-557-46057-1

One

It's hard to control your destiny while you're waiting for the bus. It's especially hard when it's a Monday and it's way too early in the morning and it's cold and gray and windy out there on the commuter-ridden sidewalks.

Twenty two year old Argus Kirkham was lining up to get on board along with all the rest of them. He was trying his best to notice nothing and no one. Who were all those people anyway? A lot of them wearing suits or nice enough clothes, likely taking their professions all seriously with their cell phones at the ready, their critical path decisions to make, their lofty goals to set and achieve. Chances were those people weren't working at some Pay'n'Pay like Argus was. Crappy job. Crappy life.

Waiting for the bus. Thoughts were swirling around in his head like the cold fog out there on the avenues. At least the pack of passengers crowding together now the bus was visible down the street was providing some kind of warmth or at least the illusion. Feet were shuffling, papers folding up as they all congealed into a heap of anticipation.

The bus came rumbling up the road, it's wheezing and lurching and grinding making pretty much the only kind of noise out in the world at that time of the morning. Argus found himself in the middle of the pack, right behind a clutch of overly perfumed ladies and right in front of a recent smoker; the combination of odious odors might have been enough to sedate a wild cat.

As the bus reached the gaggle the jostling began, although everyone knew there was plenty of room and really no hurry at all. The bus wasn't going to rush off without everyone there getting on it first. Argus felt himself tilted from the left to the right, from the back to the front, and then suddenly elbowed in the side by a stubbly old man in a pea green overcoat who pushed his face right into Argus' neck and muttered something that sounded like 'Sorry, Charlie'.

The old man pushed something into Argus' hands and then he was gone and the procession continued and Argus was two steps up and reaching for his bus pass when he realized he was holding a small cardboard box. He tried to look over his shoulder to see if he could spot the old man but there was only the smoker behind him, and a couple of large guys behind that one, and no sign of anyone outside on the sidewalk who wasn't in the boarding pack.

Argus shrugged, shifted the package to one hand and fumbled around finding his pass and flashing it at the driver, a scowling young woman who was paying no attention at all. He stuffed the bus pass back in his pocket along with the other junk he carried around in there; a few forgotten keys, an old silver ring, a tiny compass and a black plastic toy ninja for luck. He followed the seatmongers towards the rear, figuring he would probably have to be standing all the way downtown. He made it to the back door where all at once a little old lady who'd been sitting there calmly jumped up and pushed her way down the steps and outside. Argus took her seat before anyone else even noticed. The window seat was occupied by a snoring office worker, a young fellow in his early twenties also, dressed up nice in suit and tie but had forgot to comb his hair and was drooling down his chin in his sleep while his head bounced off the glass at every stop and start. The bus driver seemed to be in training. Passengers were holding on tight and Argus had to keep pushing the drooler off his shoulder as they slowly crawled down the road. In between pushes he examined the little box.

It was maybe six inches by nine and a couple inches thick, not much bigger than a paperback book. The box showed the residue of multiple usages, bits of packing tape and labels and addresses heavily blacked out with thick marker, but nothing legible remained written on any surface. The box was barely sealed with tape on either end. "It isn't mine", he thought. "I shouldn't open it", but naturally he was curious. He held it up to his ear and shook it a little just to make sure that nothing was ticking inside. He heard some tiny rattling noises inside and made some haphazard guesses like a kid on Christmas morning. Couldn't be money, he thought with a sigh. No one goes around handing out boxes of money. Or boxes of anything, for that matter.

He tried to remember the man who had shoved it at him but only came up with the pea green of the coat and the stubble and the age. No other details remained in his mind.

"I might as well open it", Argus decided. It was easy to do. The tape was old and pulled off easily. Inside were several small objects each wrapped in its own page of aged and weatherbeaten newsprint. As he carefully unfolded the items, he tried to keep them all straight on his lap, but the heaving of the bus and the jostling by his neighbor made it bothersome. After revealing a few items he decided to leave the rest for later, and put them all back together as they had been before.

He sat back in his seat and closed his eyes, shaking his head. The little he'd seen had not given him much to go on. There was a typical looking brass house key, a couple of little toy men and a couple of old cereal box tops. The remaining items were probably just as random and as meaningless. It might have been all that was left in the world that belonged to some sad homeless man. Maybe he was just passing them on, his own kind of tragic ceremonial event. Lost in the world, Argus thought, and he felt that he knew what that was like.

Two

"That's just some crazy shit", Mikael commented when he heard the story. "And believe me I know my crazy"

"I believe you", Argus replied, smiling.

They were taking a break from their shipping and receiving duties in the back room at the Pay'n'Save convenience store. Surrounded by an endless mountain of incoming and outgoing boxes, the two men huddled around a snot green card table where Argus had laid out the full contents of the mystery package. He had only barely saved it from the mischievous hands of the little neighborhood brats Karly and Kansas, who seemed to think it was their job to greet Argus with some petty thievery and make him chase them around the building practically every morning. Argus had made it a habit to carry something he didn't mind losing, some random object off the street for instance, as a decoy to protect anything else more valuable. It was Kansas who had snatched the box and pulled the usual disappearing act around the corner.

Argus could never guess where the kids would get to. They

seemed to have a new vanishing act every day. This time it was Karla who reappeared just as Argus was starting to get steamed. The child was suddenly at his side in the back parking lot, holding out the box with a blank expression in her big brown eyes. As soon as he touched it, she lifted herself on her toes and dashed away. He'd stashed the package in his cubby and spent the rest of the morning opening other boxes, counting items, checking off invoices, typing and filing away records of the items as they arrived: candy bars, Kotex, chips, frozen burritos, laundry detergent, anything and everything that filled the shelves of the local branch of the national chain of mom and pop replacement shops.

It was a stupid job. Not the thing he had in mind exactly when he'd ditched his home and family and left to start a new and different life. It was different all right, sharing a small house with five other people, none of whom he'd known when he'd moved in, working away for peanuts, coming home dead tired just to drag his ass to the bus again in the morning. What really got him was the lack of a future. Here he was only twenty two years old and he couldn't see a day beyond tomorrow.

"I like the little robots", Mikael said, picking up one of the red and black plastic toys and examining it closely. The robot was all one piece and had a smooth head, a grimace for a mouth, and peculiar round spectacles for eyes.

"It looks like a bad guy", he declared.

"No way", Argus said, "he's totally harmless"

"Bad guy", Mikael repeated, putting that one down and picking up the other, nearly identical to the first except for its yellow and blue coloring, and square spectacles instead of round.

"Good guy", Mikael pronounced.

"It's just the colors you like", Argus told him and Mikael beamed.

"Why not? What could be more natural? You see a thing you like you call it good. You see a think you don't you call it bad. So what? Who cares? You could change your mind tomorrow, call the good thing bad and the bad thing good. You could like the Lakers all of a sudden."

"I don't know about that", Argus murmured, "really, the Lakers?"

"Anything", Mikael continued. "What is like and not like? It's just made up stuff. You see something, you decide what you think of it. This is all"

"So what do you think of these?", Argus asked, holding up a couple of Bite Size Shredded Wheat cereal box box-tops. At that moment, Celestina walked by and practically shouted,

"That is not food!"

"Try it you'll like it", Mikael dared her, turning to yell after her as she brushed past him on her way to the rest room.

"I like shredded wheat", Argus said.

"So what? Who cares?", replied Mikael. "I'm sorry, did you say something?"

"What is all this?", Argus asked himself again.

Each of the items from the box were now before him. Seven old photographs, a handwritten note that was barely legible and made no sense, two toy robots, the box tops, a house key, and the newspaper wrappings themselves, which once he looked closely at noticed they were clippings, complete articles from different newspapers from different cities, different dates.

"It's either garbage or clues", Mikael suggested, picking up the photos and flipping through them briefly before tossing them back on the table.

"I would say it's most likely garbage"

"What's all this?" somebody said, and Argus and Mikael looked up to see their boss, Ahmed Atta, towering over them.

"A long story", Argus said.

"Curious", Ahmed, leaning his tall slender body over the table to get a closer look. "I'd like to hear about it"

"Some old man stuck a box in my hands while I was getting

on the bus this morning", Argus told him. "This is what was in it?"

"Where is the box now?" Ahmed asked, and Argus gestured towards the carton which was still sitting in his cubby.

"You will want to save every bit of it", Ahmed told him. "Such things do not occur in the normal flow of events"

"Tell me about it", Mikael scoffed, shaking his head. He was used to his boss's superstitious ways. Mikael had been working for Ahmed for several years by now, always sticking with his back room job and evading every possible promotion. Mikael was probably in his mid to late thirties but was very guarded about his personal life. No one at the store could tell if he was married, had a family, or even where he came from, although they all assumed it was Russia and he didn't bother to correct them. He as from the Ukraine, actually. He liked his situation now, and didn't mind putting up with nonsense like this from Ahmed. He even enjoyed it.

"You will want to see Madam Sylvia", Ahmed continued. "You will want to take her the contents exactly as they were as far as possible. Madam Sylvia will have something interesting to say about all this, I am sure"

"Madam Sylvia", Mikael laughed, "will tell you anything you want to hear as long as money is green and there is some of it to give her."

"Don't be like that, Mikael", Ahmed scolded, wagging his finger in the air. "This is something here. This isn't every day."

"Okay", Argus agreed. "I will take it to Madam Sylvia"

"Go now", Ahmed said, "or any time this afternoon. I don't mind."

"Thanks, boss", said Argus, but as Ahmed walked back into the main store room, he and Mikael exchanged glances and tried not to laugh too loudly.

"Oh Madam Sylvia", Mikael joked, imitating the boss, "look at all this crap I have. I am so very full of shit am I not?"

"You don't even know", Argus snorted.

Celestina came wading back and with her wide and swinging hips again managed to nearly topple Mikael from his rickety chair and not by accident. She tossed her hair, gestured with her hand at the mountain of work surrounding them, and taunted,

"Tell me when you're all done processing these boxes"

"One of these days I will process your big fat ass", Mikael called after her but not too loudly as the door was swinging open again, and Mr. Fontanel himself could be seen just outside it.

"Oops", Mikael muttered and hastily got up and busied himself with a box cutter. Argus wrapped the strange assorted items back up in their newspaper bundles, and stashed them away in their package, and then also got back to work. There was another hour and a half until lunch time. The trip to Madam Sylvia would have to wait. With Fontanel lurking around, it was all heads down and fingers moving.

Three

Argus didn't go see Madam Sylvia that day. Instead, he plodded through the afternoon, ripping through one box after another in a more and more mindless daze as the hours went by. Finally, without another word to anyone, he collected the package and slipped out the back door. He was not feeling especially sociable, as usual. He never had been the outgoing type. Only recently had he come to recognize how awkward that could be. He floated through the crowds in a shell of his own, barely looking outward, barely seeing the world. He would arrive home and not really know where he had been along the way.

"Home", he would think, "I guess you would have to call it that".

It was a typical house in the gloom, its three bedrooms and "utility" room not nearly enough space for the six young people who lived there. Argus wasn't even sure how he'd ended up in that place. He'd answered some ads and visited some places, ending up there. Sometimes he wondered what they thought of him. He was the largest one there, at six foot two, two hundred and twenty five pounds, with shaggy long light brown hair and the faintest beginnings of growth on his chin, large brown eyes often displaying an expression like ocean-worn glass.

The others included two nearly interchangeable frat boys, Todd and Brian, and Seth, apparently a stoner, and two of their unlikely girlfriends, Todd's Maribel and Seth's Jolene. The first two of the men were in the earliest stages of promising careers. The women were entrepreneurs, and it was really their house, from which they had started and still ran their catering business. They were determined to succeed but in the meantime required some help with the rent. Argus was certain he would not be there long. He felt completely out of place, even more there than at the store. His whole new lifestlye adventure was coming to seem like a giant mistake, but he had no other ideas. He had always lived there, in the same Spring Hill Lake, a city without any character. He was born there, grew up there, went to college there too, all that time living in the same house with his largely invisible parents and his older brother, Alex.

Five years older, Alex had moved along a long time before, leaving Argus alone, really alone in that house. He almost never saw his parents, almost never talked to them. They were there, all that time, but each one going his own way, minding his own business, never really a family. His mother and father hardly spoke to each other so it was hardly surprising they had even less to do with their son, who was never much of a talker, anyway. He had a been a bright child, quiet but perceptive, but all along the way, through school after school, through phases of youth, adolescence, into adulthood, he'd become more and more distant, more and more silent, more and more deadened and dulled. Depression. He knew that's what it was. It seemed normal, however, not something to change or to expect to be changed. He had become adjusted and accustomed to what he called 'his way'.

Arriving home, he slipped into his room, which was conveniently just inside the front door, to the left. His roommates often didn't know whether he was home or not, and most of them didn't even care. Jolene, however, who considered herself the founder and therefore the head of the household, was always on the alert. From her post in the kitchen, way in the back of the house, she could sense his arrival, and had lately decided to make an effort to penetrate his stillness. Her friend Maribel was offended by Argus' aloofness and was simply hoping that he'd go away. She preferred the liveliness of Brian and Todd, or even the simple friendliness of Seth, who at least had the common courtesy to say 'hey' and 'goodbye' and 'how are you'.

"I don't know why you bother", she called after Jolene, who was heading up the hall with a chocolate cupcake.

"Everybody needs somebody", Jolene replied to herself.

She thought of Argus as like a little brother, even though he towered over her. She gently pushed his door open and saw him seated at the little table he used for a desk. He had opened the package and once again arrayed its contents, but he was looking out the window at the quiet side street they faced.

"I thought you might like this", Jolene said quietly, and approached with the cupcake. Argus turned and looked up at her with an attempt at a smile. His arm felt heavy as if he could hardly lift it to accept the offering. He didn't. Jolene came closer and placed it on the table.

"That's quite a collection", she said. "From your childhood?"

"What?" Argus murmured, "Oh, this stuff. No. It isn't mine, or it wasn't, or maybe it still isn't. Somebody gave it to me. I don't know why"

"Somebody you know?" she asked

"No, no", it felt like effort to say, "A stranger. At the bus stop. It's strange"

"Wow", Jolene was impressed. "That's so unusual. I wonder what it means. Do you have any idea?"

"No", he said, "I really haven't thought about it much. I've just been carrying it around as if I was doing something I'm supposed to. I should've just thrown it in the garbage"

"Oh no", Jolene said. "You couldn't do that. Not without trying, at least"

"Trying what? It's just some random old junk some crazy old guy pushed into my hands."

"What if it's not?", she said. She was still standing beside the table, and now she was leaning over, trying to get a better look at the scraps of paper and the pile of photos and the toys. "What if he meant it for you, for a reason?"

"I never saw him before".

"He might have seen you. Or somebody else might have put him up to it."

"I hadn't thought about that", Argus said. They were silent for a few moments. Jolene began to feel like the intruder she was.

"Well, don't throw it away", she said, backing out towards the door. "And I'd be glad to help", she continued, "if you want, that is. It's none of my business I know but, I like puzzles, and sometimes I'm even good at them."

"Okay", Argus said. He was just waiting for her to leave, although he didn't want her to. "Oh, and thanks for the cupcake"

"You're welcome", she said, as she made her way out of the

room, and gently closed the door behind her.

"Did he say anything?" Maribel quizzed her upon her return to the kitchen.

"Uh-huh", said Jolene. "He even said thanks"

"Well, you never see that every day", Maribel shrugged, but she was ready to get back to business. They'd had a call from a customer that morning and there was plenty of work to be done.

Four

Three of the household were in the kitchen. Maribel Lewis was the public face, big hair, and booming voice of Mari-Jo Incorporated, Food Services. Her boyfriend, Todd, and his buddy Brian, were out, as usual, at the local sports bar, drinking beers and pretending to be Irish. Jolene was busying herself with food preparation. She had been to the culinary academy and spent most of her waking hours dreaming up confectionery concoctions. The two women complemented and contrasted each other completely; the silence and the roar, the taste for sweets and the nose for money. They would certainly be successful together someday and they knew it.

Seth liked to say he was in real estate. In fact he was the handyman for his parents' property management enterprise. He was too embarrassed to admit this to anyone, but the job actually suited him nicely. He was a tinkerer and a dawdler by nature, exactly what people expected from someone in his position. He was also a homebody, which is why, in the evenings his long frame was often slung across the sofa just outside the kitchen, in the utility slash living room by the back steps while the women conducted their business. He looked up with his goofy smile as Argus, appeared in the doorway.

"Hey man, what's shakin'?" he asked with his customary greeting. Argus hadn't even noticed him there. He'd been looking for Jolene.

"Oh", he stammered, "Not much, I guess. Just wanted to say. I mean, just wanted to ask. I mean, tell"

"What's up?" Jolene looked up from her mixing bowls and baking sheets.

"It's just that I wanted to say", Argus was having trouble getting the words out. "Like you were saying before. Look, I don't know what to make of that stuff, so if you really meant, if you wanted to check it out. Anyway, I'd be glad if you wanted to"

Seth and Maribel switched both their puzzled stares from Argus to Jolene, who was nodding and said to Alex,

"Thanks, I will. Do you want to bring it out here? Or leave it where it is? Either way. As soon as I get a chance I'll take another look"

"I guess somebody knows what they're talking about", Maribel put in.

"Beats the hell out of me" Seth shrugged in response.

"It's a mystery", Jolene explained as Argus still stood in the doorway, not sure what he should do next. He was halfway to turning around and walking away but the other half knew that wouldn't be right, and so he remained, awkwardly rooted to the spot.

"Some old guy came out of nowhere and gave Argus this little box, and inside it were a bunch of random things wrapped up in newspaper articles. Argus has no idea what it's all about, is that right?"

"Not a clue", Argus agreed.

"I had an old street guy come up to me one time", Seth said. "He started quoting Bible verses at me, then stuff out of the Qu'ran, and finally something out of Buddha. I was just standing there minding my own business."

"That's crazy", Maribel said.

"Yeah, I thought so too", said Seth, "but then he handed me a slip of paper, and on it was written a book and chapter and verse out of the Bible, and he told me to look it up when I got to my job."

"Did you?" Jolene asked, although she already knew the answer. He had told her this story a bunch of times before. She liked to check to see if he was going to change it. So far, he never had.

"Yeah", he continued. "I mean, I was working at the bookstore so there was a Bible. Most jobs don't have Bibles hanging around so I thought it was even weird he said to look it up when I got to work. Anyway, I did, and it was out of Ecclesiastes and it said, 'of the making of many books there is no end, and much study is a weariness of the flesh'".

"Wow", said Maribel, "you were working in a bookstore and it was a quote about books? How did he happen to have that written down on a piece of paper anyway?"

"Maybe he had a bunch of pieces of paper saved up", Argus suggested, "and picked the one that fit."

"But how did he know?" Seth asked. "Unless, I mean, I always wondered if maybe he'd seen me working at the store, but it wasn't even in that neighborhood".

"Homeless people get around", Jolene said.

"I guess so", Seth said. "It's kind of creepy if you think about it. There's people out there who could know about you, see where you go. You don't know them but they know you."

"Maybe your old guy was like that", Jolene suggested to Argus.

"Maybe", he said. "I didn't even think of that"

"I don't want to think about things like that", Maribel declared, and with her bossiest voice reminded Jolene they had work to do and that the work had to get done pretty soon. Jolene promised Argus she would come around in the morning if he didn't mind, and that gave him the excuse he needed to get away from the kitchen and get back to his room. Once he was back there, he was not happy with himself. He had actually enjoyed the little conversation. He told himself that Seth seemed like a perfectly nice and even interesting guy, and that he liked Jolene even if he didn't like Maribel, and what harm would it do to come out and stay out and get to know them all better? And since when had he become such a loner?

He couldn't answer that question. Looking back at his life it seemed he had always been like that, choosing to remain alone in his room, not even doing much except thinking and not even about anything in particular. Growing up he had shared a room with his brother. He had the bottom bunk and would stay there, under the blankets, while Alex had friends over or was just doing his stuff. Argus would peek out now and then, but never was much of a talker. Everyone thought he was smart because he was quiet, when really he had nothing to say. And then there were the long still years after Alex had left home to start his new life, and Argus was left behind to face the family that wasn't really a family, in the house that was merely there.

He was almost paralyzed by routine, dragging himself through a college degree in architecture of all things, as if he cared anything about that. He couldn't explain to himself or to anyone else the choices he'd made, the shape his life had taken. He only knew he didn't like it and he wanted it to change. He didn't know how that was going to happen. As he'd said to Jolene, he had no idea. No ideas, really, he said to himself. He knew the blankness he felt had another name, and he knew it had held him in its grip as far back as he could recall. But to make the change happen, this was why he'd chosen to move, chosen to live with strangers, to work at some job, any job. His only notion was that any change in any way, any move in any direction, would lead to somewhere in the end, and he didn't need to know where that would be, or how that would happen. It just would. It had to.

Five

Jolene Marsh had stayed up late, baking way past midnight, so she slept in in the morning, not waking up until ten. At that time she had the house to herself. Seth had mosied off to one or another of his parents' apartment buildings, Maribel had loaded up the car with the goods and headed out to make deliveries. Todd and Brian, hungover and grumpy, made their way downtown to their junior white collar gigs. Argus had been the earliest to rise and leave, huddled in the fog at the bus stop wondering if any more strangers were out there watching him.

The house was divided by a long narrow hallway which ran all the way down the middle. You walked up the front steps and entering could select from bedrooms on the right (Seth and Jolene's) and left (Argus's) , then another on the left (Maribel and Todd) across from the bathroom on the right, and then finally the kitchen on the left, utility slash living room on the right. Behind those were the pantry, enclosed sun room slash porch slash Brian's pad, and finally the back yard down the back steps. Jolene had lived there first, with an entirely different set of roommates, and had accumulated the current set beginning with Maribel. She was more or less satisfied with the current situation, although if she was pressed she would admit that she'd rather that Brian in particular was not there, and that they had no financial need for Argus' presence either.

Brian was the official slob of the house, and otherwise was practically Todd's shadow, following him everywhere, liking everything he liked and doing everything he did. Jolene didn't have much patience for people she called 'clones'. On the other hand, he paid the rent and was rarely actually in the house, so it was not intolerable. Seth thought the pair were 'entertaining' but she knew he was easily amused. He would talk to them as if they were one person, directing the conversation first to one and then to the other no matter which one responded, and they never caught on, which drove Maribel crazy.

With everyone out of the house, Jolene enjoyed the peace. She wandered up and down the hall, from bathroom to coffee to bedroom to porch, until finally remembering her plan to look at Argus' collection. She entered his room with a little nostalgia - it had been her room on two separate prior occasions. It still contained her old furniture - the bed, the dresser, even the table and chair had been hers. The articles were still spread out on the table as Argus had left them. Sitting down and looking them over, she was struck first by how neatly he'd arranged them. After that, she could make nothing of it. The photographs were from different cameras, from different eras, and pictured either people or buildings, or people in front of buildings. If Argus didn't know what they were about, she certainly knew even less. If they had been people he knew, wouldn't he have said so? But he hadn't really said anything either way.

The newspaper articles also seemed completely random, and were from different newspapers at different times. Some of the stories themselves also concerned buildings, but others did not. What a mess, she thought, and she wished she had more to go on, that she'd asked Argus more questions about it, that he was there now to ask. She knew he had studied architecture, so there might be some sense in the pictures and articles about buildings. Two of the articles were about buildings that were destroyed. She remembered one of the stories, about the Sea Dragons football stadium, and how it had to be torn down even though it was almost brand new. There had been some odd rumors about it but the newspaper article was only reporting the fact of it, that the stadium had come down on schedule and without incident. There was nothing else about football or stadiums in any of the other stories or photographs.

She was determined to find a link, or at least a clue. The two toy robots meant nothing to her, and didn't seem in any way related to anything else. The handwritten note was nonsense and nearly impossible to read. She could only make out a few words: elevator, paddle, foreign, averted, quicksand. Nonsense. She set the note aside. The only item she hadn't looked at yet were the two box tops from Bite Size Shredded Wheat. Those were the first genuine clue, for it said on the backs that they could be redeemed for a magic secret decoder ring. Jolene nearly jumped up with excitement and relief, but she looked again and saw that the offer had expired nearly a decade ago.

"Oh my God", she said to herself. "I've got nothing. Nothing at all. Back to the newspapers, I guess."

Besides the two demolition stories there was a book review, an obituary notice, something about some rich kid's birthday party, a story about someone who was kidnapped and held hostage in a secret room in a house, and, lastly, a piece about a corrupt politician going to jail. There was nothing about any one story that seemed to have anything to do with any other story, and nothing that seemed to connect to the photographs either. She had thought at first that maybe the buildings in the stories were matched by buildings in the photos but they clearly weren't. The people in the photos also seemed to have no relation to the stories or each other. There must be something, she thought, something that ties at least two of these things together. Probably the house key. But she knew she was only guessing wildly.

She was as stumped as she had ever been, more so even. She was someone who could do those word jumbles in record times, someone who could do jigsaw puzzles almost blindfolded. She thought she could see the patterns in anything, but here she was drawing a blank. Among the photos was one of an old woman all dressed in black, walking through a garden. Another was of two young boys playing on a seesaw in a park. There was an old photo of a young family - husband, wife, young boy and girl - posing in front of a rundown ramshackle cottage surrounded by a high cyclone fence. Another photo was of a brand new office building, but the name on the sign in the front, 'Spring River', did not match the one in the newspaper story, a building called 'Fulsom

Towers' which had collapsed and was described as being much taller than the one in the photo. Another photo was of an anonymous one story building in an office park somewhere, with two identical red cars parked in front but no indication of where it was. The last were a photo of a crowded corner produce market in the city, and two old men in a park who appeared to be playing cards.

Still nothing. No matter how hard she looked, she didn't see anything. Dejected, she left the items as they were, and left the room. Several times during the day she returned, but she didn't get any further. She even went as far as to call the cereal company to ask about the secret decoder rings, but that was a conversation that didn't get far. The startled customer service representative could only reply that he didn't know what to tell her. Promotions that old were completely forgotten.

Six

As he tooled home down the boulevard, Seth McDuffie thought again about how his little yellow Carmen Ghia convertible had won him Jolene's heart. She had been standing on a downtown sidewalk getting ready to cross the street when she saw him pull up to the stop sign and actually come to a complete stop to let her cross. She came right over to him and he'd thought it was to thank him for stopping, or then maybe secondarily she'd thought he was cute but no, she wanted to ask about the car, what kind it was, how old it was, where he'd gotten it, how much it cost. She had so many questions all at once, so he just said "why don't you get in and we'll go somewhere and talk about it", and amazingly enough, she did.

They drove over to the Seal Rock Cafe and he told her everything she could possibly want to know about the car. By the end of that date the car was practically hers, seeing as he was going to be her new boyfriend and was probably going to move in to her place and he would probably let her drive it, which was really at the bottom of it all. A pretty good deal, he told himself. After all, he'd found it in a junkyard and gotten it almost for free, put it back together himself on evenings and weekends as he scraped together the money for parts and paint and wheels. Took him two years almost, and ever since then that car had been his baby, like a baby even with all the care and maintenance and attention it required. And he did let Jolene drive it. Hell, if that was the price of admission it was worth it, well worth it. The way he saw it, he'd never before even met what he called 'a woman of quality'. He couldn't pin down what that meant, only that he knew it when he saw it and Jolene was definitely it.

The garage at their house was unusual in that it was actually used for parking a car inside. It might have been the only garage on the block that wasn't a bedroom or den or storage bin inside. And the automatic door opener even worked, and Seth used it and drove the tiny car right in. Getting out, he walked around the car twice, inspecting the coat and the chrome to make sure it was still in perfect shape. Sometimes he almost hated taking it out into the wide and dirty world. You deserve better, he said to the car, a world where there is no traffic and there is no smog, not even your own, where you can drive a million miles on nothing but the good sweet air. He was still dreaming of inventing a combustion engine that combusted nothing at all. Upstairs he heard the sound of voices coming from the front of the house. He recognized Jolene's and headed toward the sound like a moth to fire.

Coming into the front bedroom he saw her pacing the floor, while new roomie Argus sat on the only chair in front of the little table and seemed to be staring out the window.

"Hey man, what's shakin'?" Seth said.

"Hi honey", Jolene skipped over and stood on her toes to give him a light hug and a peck on the cheek before tripping off.

"We're stumped", she announced as if that were a victory.

"Oh yeah, the mystery", he remembered and he walked over to where Argus was now looking up at him.

"So, this is the famous pile of junk", he said, looking down at the table.

"Seems that's exactly what it is", Argus replied.

"Funny", Seth said. "Someone sure went to some trouble to put that all together. Did you say everything was wrapped up in those newspaper articles?"

"Yeah", Argus told him.

"A couple of those articles have the dates written on them in pen", Seth said, thinking aloud. He had a habit of doing that.

"I guess so", Argus said. "Think that means something?"

"You'd have to go with the idea that everything means something here."

"You're right", Jolene declared. She stood next to Seth with her arm around his waist. "I've just been looking at the big picture trying to see a general pattern."

"You might want to take it piece by piece", Seth suggested. He picked up one of the photos, the one with the two boys in the playground. Turning it over he muttered,

"Someone wrote the date on this one too"

Argus turned over all the rest of the photos and pointed at them. The others nodded. Dates were written on the backs of each photo, not with the same pen, and not by the same hand, but each one was dated.

"All the articles have dates too", Seth said. "I only noticed the one that was written in ink; the others have their date from the paper itself."

"It doesn't look like any of the dates are the same", Jolene said, now studying that item.

"That might be your pattern", Seth suggested.

"I'll re-arrange them", Argus said. "We need more space", and Jolene said,

"Let's take them out to the kitchen".

Argus picked up the pile and the three moved off as she'd indicated. Seth decided to make some tea so he was getting that together while Argus and Jolene spread out the photos and articles again and started putting them in chronological order.

Seth's guess proved interesting and soon they had formed two lines of seven items each. Jolene decided to make a list that she could walk around with. She wrote down the following:

August 6, 1986 - story, Harold Miner III's 23rd birthday party

March 28, 1988 - photo, two old men in park playing cards

November 11, 1989 - story, book review of 'The Witchcraft of Positive Thinking"

July 11, 1991 - photo, neighborhood produce market

March 2, 1993 - story, death of a woman named Cyrilla Pak

October 23, 1994 - photo, two boys on seesaw at playground

June 14, 1996 - story, city mayor convicted of bribery charges

February 4, 1998 - story, collapse of Fulsom Towers office building

September 27, 1999 - photo, family in front of fence and house

May 19, 2001 - photo, two red cars in an office park

January 9, 2003 - story, Sea Dragons Stadium demolished

August 31, 2004 - photo, Spring River office building

April 23, 2006 - photo, old woman in black in a garden

December 14, 2007 - story, kidnapping and secret room in house.

"Well, that's different at least", Seth said, arriving at the kitchen table with a pot and three cups.

"Different and yet the same", Argus shrugged.

"Is there anything about any of those dates that mean anything to you?" Seth asked.

"Just the first one", Argus replied. "That was the day I was born. August 6, 1986"

"No way!", Jolene nearly shouted. "That's got to mean something!"

"Yup", Seth agreed. "Maybe we can say that this thing was definitely intended for you."

"Maybe", Argus said. "It would be a hell of a coincidence otherwise."

"It's a start", Jolene said. "Now we're getting somewhere."

Seven

Jolene made meticulous copies of her list and ceremoniously handed them to Argus and Seth with instructions to carry them around in case inspiration struck. They had made no further progress that night, and Argus had packed up the contents and put them away in his room to avoid any problems from Brian or Todd or Maribel. That was Jolene's idea. She didn't really trust the others to treat this as anything other than a joke. She had visions of tearage, tramplage and crumplage and other unkind treatment of the relics at the hands of the two in particular she referred to as 'the beasts'.

"Better safe than sorry", she said as she helped Argus arrange the items in their package and stow them away in a drawer.

Throughout the following day, after she once again had the house to herself, having dispatched Maribel to a customer site visit and shuffled Seth off to do something, anything, anywhere, she periodically stopped into Argus' room for a visual inspection of the package. In between those episodes she studied her copy of the list, and by the end of the day she had reached some very interesting conclusions. She found herself shelling peanuts out of restlessness and impatience for the men to return so that she could share her discoveries.

Seth, meanwhile, was investigating nothing at all. He loped from one building to the next, checking in and checking up. As usual, he had a lot of long, friendly conversations with various tenants, most of whom were in love with him to some degree. He was just one of those people. Whatever it was that he had, agreeableness, kindness, confidence, casualness, all of that together with a goofy grin and a seeming empathy that may have been more apparent than real, he was never at a loss for company. It could be a problem sometimes, when certain tenants would phone in faux problems just so Seth would come around and visit. He never seemed to mind or even catch on. The plumbing somehow fixed itself by the time he arrived, but sure, a lemonade sounded fine. That hole in the wall that needed patching seemed to have been delicately placed there to ensure not only his presence but also that he wouldn't be put out too much. And so his days were filled with friends and acquaintances and hows-it-shakins and hows-it-hangins and a nod and a smile and a bit of tinkering here and there.

Mr and Mrs McDuffie, his parents, were also his biggest fans.

They were a well-suited pair of near-sighted balding and bright orange pants suits that had somehow managed to manage a collection of decent little buildings in decent little neighborhoods, averaging six to ten units apiece. They owned only one, along with their house. The rest they just ran for others. Mister, the father, had some of Seth's traits, the social ease and gregariousness. From the mom he inherited the others, the seeming lack of self-awareness and tendency to drift through life. It was cool. Everything was always cool. And once in awhile a thought crossed his mind, like the thought that he had driving home through the city, the thought that made him pull over and pull out the list and nod and smile and think to himself that won't Jolene be surprised that he figured this out by himself.

For his part, Argus was more concerned about who might be watching him walk to the bus stop, wait at the bus stop, and get on the bus. There was no one as far as he saw. Maybe they took the day off, he said to himself. Just my luck. The one time I'm looking there's nobody there. The whole thing was making him nervous. That the sequence of items began on the day he was born. What could it possibly mean? As badly as he wanted the thing to be random and pointless, the harmless obsession of a crazy old coot, it was harder now to think that it could be. So he tried not to think about it at all. Nothing doing.

Ahmed at work kept annoying him about Madam Sylvia. Mikael kept bringing it up too. Argus tried to say as little as possible, but he did spill the thing about the day he was born, and he mentioned the list, and then Mikael had to see it. Mikael practically tore it out of his hands and made off with it into the bathroom. He stayed in there for awhile. Argus was at least glad that he'd left the originals at home. God only knew what Mikael was doing in there. When he came out, the first thing he said was

"How old are you now, twenty two is that right?" and when Argus said "yes", Mikael shouted

"I knew it. I knew it"

"This, my friend", he said, waving the list around in the air, "is a very most interesting puzzle. What is most intriguing of all is the date that is NOT on the list. Do you know what I mean?"

Argus shook his head "no".

"What is not on this list is the very last day, the finality of the sequence. Look, my dear Argus, just look", and he pulled Argus over to him and held the list in front of his face.

"Day one, we know that, is the day you were born. The significance of the photographs or other news items with dates, of this I know nothing. I do not know if there is any meaning at all in those things. Probably yes. I would say yes most certainly likely. But what that inference would be, again I can't say. The next date on the list, do you see? Exactly six hundred days from the first. And the one after that? Six hundred more days."

"Six hundred days?" Argus wasn't sure he was hearing correctly. "What's so important about six hundred days."

"I have no idea", Mikael replied, "but six hundred days and exactly is the interval between each and every date on this list. I did all the math. Six hundred days and precisely. Now, do you follow?"

"I guess so", Argus said. He was trying to look at the dates and do the math by himself in his head, but six hundred days is a hard one to figure. It's more than a year, but less than two. It doesn't make sense in terms of any typical sequence. There was nothing about six hundred days that seemed special. Mikael seemed to be reading his thoughts.

"What's special", he declared, "about the six hundred days is that if you take six hundred days, and you add it up fourteen times, and it just happens to be that fourteen is the number of objects with dates on your list ... that the very last day on the calendar will be the same as the very first day. In short, your next birthday, when you will turn twenty three."

"Twenty three?" Argus was feeling light-headed. Wasn't the first article, dated on the day he was born, a story about somebody's twenty third birthday? And now Mikael's telling him that the date in the sequence after the last date on the list would fall on his own twenty-third? The likelihood of a random act of wildness was less and less all the time. It kind of spoiled the surprise when he finally got home, that Seth and Jolene had both arrived at the same discovery. Each of them wanted to get all the glory and credit but instead all three of them now had the same set of facts.

"It's still pretty cool", Seth pronounced.

"We're definitely on the trail now", said Jolene, but wherever that trail might be leading was still just as much a mystery as ever.

Eight

Argus had promised Ahmed that he would indeed take the package to Madam Sylvia, and since Ahmed had given him the morning off - with pay - to do just that, he did just that the next morning. First he armed himself with a worthless paperback book called 'What To Worry About And How', just in case the treacherous Karly and Kansas were lying in wait for him at the corner. They were, and they took the bait, sneaking up from behind him and snatching the book right out of his hand, then shooting off around the corner, where they hid for who knows how long because he didn't chase after them at all. Instead, he crossed the street, took the package out from under his jacket where he'd been hiding it, and entered Madam Sylvia's psychic storefront.

Sylvia had been in business at that very location for many, many years, and yet it seemed she never aged. She could hardly have been more than thirty. Old-timers were convinced she was actually over a hundred, but kept her youthful appearance due to some very evil magic. They were convinced that babies' blood had been involved at some point. Sylvia herself chalked it up to genetics. After all, her mother had lived to be ninety and even until the end never looked any older than sixty, sixty one. In fact, she had inherited the business from her mother, who was also named Madam Sylvia, so it was natural for people to think she had been there forever.

The little shop was exactly as you imagine it to be, for precisely that reason. When you go to a psychic, you expect certain things. Crystal balls, tarot cards, incense, red velvet drapes, and so on. The Madams Sylvia lair was not lacking in any of these finishing touches. Sylvia herself would have preferred something more like a psychiatrist's office, with prints of famous paintings and understated wallpaper, but she understood her market and her clientele. If it's hokey they want, it's hokey they'll get, she sighed.

Business was never slow, another fact that continually surprised her. It was understandable that people are afraid of the unknown, and the future is by definition - or at least by our common experience - unknown, although she understood that from the vantage point of the general theory of relativity, the future might be perceived to be simultaneous with all other points in time depending on your location and velocity within the space time continuum. Science, and especially quantum mechanics, had helped her understand her own particular talents.

She even had a master's degree in astrophysics from the University of Leeds. The truth of the matter was that she was indeed psychic. The future was not an unknown to her eyes. It was instead a rather dreadful bore. Just as you or I can predict the destination of one ant moving along in a trail of ants, even though the ant itself might have no idea where it's going, so it was with Sylvia and the vast majority of her customers. They presented their futures to her as plainly as the noses on their faces. She had never been married. She had considered it once.

She had let herself feel that she had fallen in love with a cashier from a neighborhood bookstore. He had visions of a soft and gentle future, settling down as the owner of a cozy little store in a small touristy town, living on postcards, trinkets and mysteries, while she had her own little office in a little back room if only to keep her occupied and content. She had to admit that she almost went through with it, but there was always the problem of her mom.

Dead as she was, the old Madam Sylvia would not go away, appearing to her daughter practically daily, butting right into her business. She was liable to show up any time, day or night, and start right in with complaining. There was way too much noise. It was too quiet. Too cold or too hot. The dead are never comfy it seemed. She always wore that old blue dress. The one she was married in. The one she was buried in too. She would stand in the corner by the potted palm, and talk louder and louder until she was sure she was heard.

Mama Sylvia made such a fuss over the quiet cashier, pestering her daughter about his dirty little habits, describing the horrible children they would certainly have, and generally making such a nuisance of herself that the only way the younger one could get her to stop bothering her was to make a deal. For her part she promised she would not marry the boy. In return her mother was only allowed to badger her on weekends, Saturdays between seven and nine in the morning, to be precise. Sylvia never regretted the deal, and she didn't bother to tell her mother that she was never going to go through with it anyway. She also never told her that the dead are lousy fortune tellers.

Argus didn't have to wait long in the gaudy and predictable

waiting room. Sylvia had been expecting him, and soon ushered him into the main chamber. She had him sit down across the small round black-draped table and studied his face for a few moments in silence. Argus was holding the package in his lap but was waiting for her to speak first.

"Something happened to you", she finally said. Argus looked puzzled and didn't reply.

"When you were a small child", Sylvia said. "Something unusual happened to you, but you don't know what it was, do you?" Argus shook his head.

"No", she nodded, "you don't even remember". She paused and was silent again for awhile. "Listen to me", she continued. "You have been touched by the infinite. Do you know what that means?"

Again, he was at a loss for words. He had no idea what she was talking about.

"Try to remember", she went on. "It was ... well, I cannot say exactly what it was, but you have been marked."

"My brother says I almost drowned when I was two", he suggested, but Sylvia shook his head.

"There is nothing of the infinite about death", she replied, muttering more to herself than to him.

"Nothing could be less so. This was more like the opposite", she whispered.

"I cannot say exactly", she repeated, more loudly. "Anyway, you have brought me something to look at, I believe." Argus put the package on the table, and began to tell her about it but she raised her hand to silence him.

"I know all about it", she said. "Our friend Ahmed has already told me your story. Now, let me take a look at the objects".

Argus watched in silence as she unwrapped the items - for he had put them back together as they had originally appeared - and set them on the table very carefully. While she was doing so she kept murmuring to herself, words that sounded like "nonsense" and "silly" and "really, now".

"You know of course that these are just clues", she looked up and told him.

"It's a riddle, a puzzle."

"We've guessed that much already", he agreed.

"We?" she said quizically. "Yes, of course, you have friends."

"Not really friends", Argus said, and immediately he wondered why he'd said that. He wanted them to be his friends, all of them. Why am I so afraid? he asked himself. He always assumed that no one would like him, that he could never be good enough to even be somebody's friend. Why do I have this idea? he wondered.

"A pattern that leads up to something", she said, "or maybe not some thing, but some where and some when. Yes, all of it leads up to a place and a time. You will figure it out, but the time will be soon."

"Yes", he replied. "My birthday is in less than two weeks, and according to the pattern, that's when it - whatever it is - is supposed to happen."

"You will figure it out", she continued, holding up one of the robots. "Of course, some of these clues are more cryptic than others."

"Do you know?" he asked her. "Can you tell me what it's all about?"

"No", she declared abruptly, and began carelessly stuffing the items back into the box. "I can tell you no more, except maybe this." She stopped, holding up the newspaper book review.

"Don't bother reading that book. It is crap", and she laughed as she put it away in the package.

"There is no witchcraft", Sylvia said, "not of positive thinking or anything else. Witchcraft is bullshit. Forget about that. Just follow the clues if you can"

"Thanks", Argus said, feeling dejected. This had been no use at all. He stood and picked up the package, sticking it back in his jacket so the kids couldn't get to it.

"Try to remember", Sylvia called after him as he started walking away. "Ask your family about it"

"I don't have a family", he replied, not turning around, "not one that matters in any case."

"Try to remember", she repeated more loudly as he walked out the door and closed it behind him. Yeah, I'll try to remember, he said to himself, remember a life where nothing happened ever, not to me, not to anyone, ever. When he crossed the street, Kansas and Karly were standing there pouting, holding out the stupid book they'd stolen from him earlier, trying to taunt him to chase them, but he just waved them away and went in to work.

Nine

When Argus told Mikael and Ahmed most of what Madam Sylvia had said and not said, Ahmed was satisfied, but Mikael merely grunted,

"At least she didn't charge you. She didn't, did she?"

"No", Argus replied.

"I guess it was on the house."

"You got what you paid for", Mikael said. "Still, she might be on to something about the some where and the some when. I got an idea", and he went off to rummage around in his jacket while Argus waited patiently. Mikael returned with a city bus map and offered it to Argus.

"You can keep it", he said. "What I would do is find all the buildings and the places in the photos and the newspapers, every where there is an address of any kind mentioned or even shown, and mark it down on this map. Maybe there will be a pattern you can see."

"Okay", Argus said, dubiously. He accepted the map and was about to put it away when Mikael snatched it back, and opened it up on the shipping table and marked a spot with indelible blue ink.

"This I know for one thing", Mikael declared. "Where the old football stadium was, right here", and he proudly showed off his work to Argus.

"When they tore this thing down, everyone was shaking their heads. Still are. It was something that made no sense. Almost brand new billion dollar facility. Why would he do that, they asked. But that Fulsom guy who built it, nobody asks him any questions. He's so rich they said he must have had good reason."

"I remember", Argus nodded. "There's something in there about a place called Fulsom Towers too", he added, looking again at the package. "Must be the same guy"

"Anything worth owning, he owns it, people say", Mikael said. "Well, anyway",  and he handed the map back to Argus.

"Keep it", he repeated. "I have another one at home. I don't know why but I do", and he laughed as he walked away. Throughout the long afternoon, Argus busied himself with opening boxes and processing inventory. It was the kind of mindless work he seemed to need. Nothing to bother the brain. Nothing to worry about and how. It was not until he got home that he had to think again about anything. It was Jolene who prompted him. She was waiting at the door for whichever of the two arrived first, Argus or Seth. Seeing it was Argus, she immediately asked him for the package and when he gave it to her, she dashed off to the kitchen, where she'd earlier that day installed a color copier she'd borrowed from someone for the day.

"I figured if I made a couple of sets", she shouted over the roar of the machine, "then each of us could have one and we wouldn't have to worry about losing the originals or bothering you if in case like maybe I wanted to look at something in the middle of the day like I did today or the middle of the night like Seth last night"

Argus was standing there in the hallway kitchen door, his

customary position lately. He felt as if entering the room would be intruding on her space. Sometimes he sort of slid on by in order to get to the living room, because there was no other route, and sometimes he only stood there thinking about sliding on by, but too shy and too inwardly panicked to make the move. The problem was, he was worried he might be developing a tremendous crush on Jolene. At the same time, he was beginning to feel that Seth was maybe the person he liked the best of all the people he'd ever known. It was a weird combination, and being all bottled up the way he was, he had no idea how to deal with it. Mostly he figured he'd stay in his room and try and avoid them both, but that was becoming more difficult each day. He wanted to be with them, and they seemed to want to be with him too.

"I was thinking of a plan", Jolene was still talking, "where we would split up the clues, and each take a bunch, and work on them separately. What do you think about that?" There was total silence as Argus didn't realize she was talking to him. She repeated her idea.

"Oh", he finally said, "I guess so. Yeah, it makes sense."

Just then Seth arrived home and got caught up on the conversation quickly. Since he asked, Argus told them all about his visit to Madam Sylvia, and showed them the bus map Mikael had marked up.

"That's an awesome idea", Seth said enthusiastically.

"Which one?" Jolene asked, favoring her own.

"All of them. Both of them. Everything", Seth said, gauging from her tone that he needed to scramble.

"Finding the spots. Marking the map. Splitting it up."

"You could take the buildings", Jolene said, "since you know about that. And I could take the people."

"People?" Argus was puzzled.

"I mean the photos that have people in them", she said. "I will try and find out where they are."

"And I can find those offices", Seth said.

"Okay", Argus just wanted to be agreeable. He didn't know what he would do. Maybe he wouldn't even have an assignment.

"You can take the rest", Jolene said, speaking to Argus. "At least for starters that is."

She was already handing out copies in piles. Argus didn't know what she meant by "the rest". She was already sorting through her own copy, pulling out the photos with the men in the park, the boys on the playground, the family in front of the house. She gestured to Seth the photos and articles that he should assign to himself, and he fumbled through his own pile to match all the ones that she showed him. They were so busy organizing and negotiating their way through the papers that they didn't notice Argus, slipping away, taking his own pile along with the package and heading back into his room. Once there he sat down on his bed, and sighed.

Something once happened to me, he remembered her saying. That was the part he hadn't told anyone, not Ahmed, not Mikael, not Seth or Jolene. Maybe she knew what it was and wouldn't tell. Maybe I should go back, and ask her again, but he knew that he wouldn't. Maybe, he thought to himself. Maybe call Alex. Maybe he'd know. So many times lately he'd wanted to call, but prevented himself. Now at least he had a pretext, something to talk about, but Alex would laugh at him, saying, 'so, you went to see a fortune teller and she said some crazy shit, what do you know?'. Alex never took anything as seriously as Argus did. It was always that way, so he couldn't call his brother, who was the only other person who could possibly know what it was. If it even was anything. Nothing ever happened to me, he said to himself. Except now.

Ten

Jolene had her mind made up, and when she had her mind made up, there was nothing that was going to stand in the way. By early the next morning she had cleared out the house, dispatching Maribel on a mission to re-visit former customers in the hopes of drumming up business, and organizing Seth to get going as well. She informed him that she would drive him to his first job, then take his car out and about to follow up on some hunches. Seth, realizing this was part of the deal, reconciled himself to taking the bus between work sites the rest of the day.

Jolene's plan was simple but inefficient. She had stayed up late with a magnifying glass, minutely inspecting her selected photos for any possible hints of location, and she believed she had found a few. She had her own city map showing all of the parks and playground, and had decided on a route that would take her to the more likely ones first, which meant starting nearer the outskirts and working her way in to the city center. She had not noticed any tall buildings visible in any of the photos, so she had made the assumption they were not near downtown. The city was not the largest, but once she was on the road she realized she was in for a long day, and once she had visited the first few parks, it began to dawn on her that her plan might not be the best after all. It seemed that ever little park had its grassy area with its picnic tables, and every other one had one of those contemporary plastic playgrounds with the sandbox pit and the climbing structure. There was no map of playground details she could look at. One of them was bound to have the seesaw in the picture, unless, of course, the photo was from some other place entirely, in which case the search was even more hopeless. As for the house with the family in front, already she knew this was probably impossible.

She had found few clues in the photo, no street signs, no giveaway background objects other than a plane perhaps landing at an airport, which would only narrow it down to a pretty large neighborhood. There were areas in the town where cyclone fences surrounding a yard were not uncommon, but from the photo it looked like that one was temporary, being held in place by cinder blocks, so it was probably long gone, considering the photo was dated long since. By noon she had covered a lot of ground and was in no mood for going home empty handed. It occurred to her that maybe she was inconveniencing Seth by taking away his car all day, but she didn't allow herself to dwell on that.

She had checked off a lot of parks in one entire quadrant of the city, so that could be taken as progress, right? And parking had been easy so far. She had to laugh at that thought. Most of these parks were completely deserted, except for the occasional nanny and charge. She kept plugging away. She had brought along a notebook and was keeping meticulous notes of locations and structures, and had begun to feel like a sort of inspector. This was work that would certainly come in handy, like never, she thought. She could publish Jolene's Handy Guide to City Patches of Grass. Or maybe that wasn't such a terrible idea. It might make for a magazine article, which was something she had always wanted to do.

She was thinking about that and looking over her notes when she walked by the men playing cards in the park. She jotted down something about tables and seats, considering adding a sort of rating system to judge parks by, when she stopped and turned and stared and nearly dropped everything. It was the same two old men. It was the same two old men in the very same spot wearing the very same clothes doing the very same thing as they were in the photo. The photo that was dated more than twenty years earlier. She pulled out her color copy and checked. Identical. She had to move over just a few feet to get the exact angle as there was in the picture. Fortunately she had brought her own camera, and took several pictures of her own while the men just went on with their game, not noticing her.

These weren't simply old men. They were very old men. They would have to be at least in their nineties or older by now if the date on the photo was right. Jolene had to find out. She walked over to them and clearing her throat tried to get their attention. They still didn't notice.

"Excuse me", Jolene said, in a normal tone of voice, and when that didn't work she repeated herself louder.

"Excuse me!", but the men didn't hear or didn't seem to. She put her notebook down in the middle of the table, next to the pile of cards they were drawing from. The old man in blue took a card from the deck, held it up to his hand and discarded it onto the notebook. The other man drew and kept the card drawn, discarding another instead. Jolene was getting annoyed. She grabbed the deck and the notebook and took a step back away from the table. The old man in blue reached his hand out to draw and finding the pile missing, looked up at his partner and quietly drawled,

"Roy, where's the deck?"

"It was setting right there", Roy replied in the same easy manner. "Maybe it fell off to the ground." The old man in blue sort of leaned in his chair and looked around at the ground.

"It ain't there", he declared.

"Well it's got to be somewhere", Roy said, and he too wagged his head to the side and made a cursory glance before shrugging and saying, "Guess we're done for the day"

"Guess we are", said the old man in blue. The two old men struggled to rise up from the chairs but failed to get to their feet. They sat back down again and sighed in unison.

"Hello?" Jolene bent down and put her face right up in front of the man who was Roy. He still didn't see her. She reached out and put her hand on his shoulder, half expecting her hand to pass right through as if Roy was a ghost, but he wasn't. He was real but still did not acknowledge her presence.

"Oh for Christ's sake", she said, and she put the deck down right back where it was on the table. It was a few moments before the old man in blue said,

"Oh shoot, there it is. It's right there."

"What is right there?", Roy asked.

"The deck, on the table. Right where it was."

"Oh", replied Roy, "I thought that you said it was missing."

"I must have just missed it".

"Well you are getting old", Roy joked and attempted to laugh, but the effort was painful and nearly took all of his breath. The old man in blue took a card from the deck and brought it up to his hand, inspected it for a minute, then discarded it on to the table.

"Ain't having no luck", he declared. Jolene backed away, and took several more photos. Back in the car, she marked down the park on her map. She decided that that was enough for one day and drove off to look for Seth, to tell him the news, and give back the car.

Eleven

Organized, methodical, determined, and totally freaked out, Jolene tracked her boyfriend down at what he liked to call "building number two" in the Martinsgate section of town. There, Seth was engaged in customer relations with Mister Havenaard, a retired sailor who enjoyed telling tall tales. Seth was leaning against a lamp post on the sidewalk nodding as "The Captain" related a genuine marvel that occurred way back when at a time when the teller was probably not even born yet. Nevertheless, he claimed, it was true. He had seen things. He could tell you. A man who had died a few days before walked right up the street where the young Havenaard was playing.

"I must have been four or maybe five at the time", the sailor said. "That man was looking around as if he was lost. I watched him as he stopped in front of each house and stood there and stared. When he came up to my family's house, I asked him if he was looking for something."

"He didn't even see me", Havenaard went on. "Just kept going right on. I told him where he lived. I said 'hey Mister your house's right there' and I pointed, but he didn't hear. He walked just in that way, stopped each time, right up the block, and then he reached the corner, and then he was gone."

"He turned?" Seth wanted to know.

"Turn? Nothing. No turning. Just gone. Poof. Just like that."

"Wow", Seth said, "that's pretty wild."

"It's a crazy place", the sailor replied. "I seen more than that around there."

"Where?"

"Here", the man said, "Spring Hill Lake. There's parts of it I wouldn't even go nowadays."

"Yeah", Seth agreed, "some pretty bad neighborhoods. Every city's got 'em"

"Not like this", Havenaard told him. "I know what I've seen."

Jolene came honking up and screeched to a halt beside Seth.

She called out,

"Come on, get in, it's important", and shifted impatiently while Seth made his typical drawn-out goodbyes to the Captain. When he finally piled into the passenger seat, Jolene screamed off down the street, talking a mile a minute. She told him all about the old men in the park and to Seth it sounded familiar, like a story his sailor friend would tell. He let her vent until done. She drive right back there to show him, but of course when they arrived, there were no old men, or anyone at all in the area.

"Ive got pictures", she told him and he said,

"Wow, that's cool."

"Cool?" Jolene asked. "Is that all you got?"

"Well, it is pretty cool", he replied. "It must have seemed like the old photo came alive just like that."

"I took pictures", Jolene repeated.

"Listen", said Seth, when he finally got a chance to tell her. "I found something myself."

He unfolded his own bus map and laid it out on the table and sat down right where Roy had been sitting.

"I figured I might need it. Since you had the car, I had to take the 46 and the 63 but I guess I got turned around and went the wrong way. Anyway it's a good thing I did because I was just sitting there looking out the window when we went by that Spring River office building, the one in the photo from 2004. So I marked it down on the map. Look, it's up here."

"What are those other black circles?", she asked, checking over his map.

"That one down there is your park", he replied. "Then further up, the Spring River building. Then another couple blocks further and across the street, that's where the Fulsom Towers building fell down. You notice the pattern?"

"There's two on Visitation Street", Jolene said. "And the one at the end, that's the stadium, right? I remember that place. It's on a different street, though, and so's my park."

"It's not the street", Seth pointed out. "It's the map. All four of those places are on the same bus route, the 63 Venezia line. See? It goes here, and then here", he followed its path with his finger.

"Oh my God", Jolene said, "Maybe we could find all the other places too!"

"Just follow the bus", Seth said with a grin.

They did. Jolene drove the whole length of the line, and then they switched places and Seth drove it back, but they didn't find anything else. The 63 Venezia carved a diagonal path from the northeast to the southwest of the square-shaped city. Along the way it passed through city center, and on either side a variety of residential neighborhoods and local shopping districts. At the far northern end the line ended abruptly in front of a vast, rubble-filled vacant lot which was formerly the site of the Sea Dragons football stadium. At the other end it trickled to a halt in a series of twists and turns through the rundown harbor area known as Old Town.

Jolene's park was on the edge of that neighborhood, where Visitation Boulevard turned into Settlement Drive. It was here that the city was founded, more than two hundred years earlier, along the banks of the Wetford River. The harbor was only used now by drifters who squatted in old houseboats, by weekend warriors who drove out there from shiny new condos to sail in their mini-yachts, and by locals who clung to the old ways. You could still find a bakery there, one that actually baked bread. Maybe it was too much to expect, Seth reflected, and maybe my so-called discovery was only a fluke. After all, it was hardly strange that the two tall office buildings would be located in the heart of downtown on one of the busiest streets. All of the tall buildings were in that vicinity. Jolene was still buzzing about her amazing find, and initially rejected Seth's notion that maybe the date on the photo was wrong, that maybe the photo was recent. In that case perhaps it wasn't so strange for a pair of old pals to be out playing cards in the park, but Jolene countered with 'why would anyone go to the trouble of putting the wrong date on a photo', to which Seth could only reply that 'why would anyone go to the trouble of putting that whole package together'. It seemed to him that the date merely fit the six hundred day sequence.

"But in that case", Jolene said, "why should we believe that any of the dates are correct?"

"Maybe they're not", he replied.

After a long afternoon of tracing the route without further success, Seth and Jolene finally went home, where Maribel was waiting with news of a huge new catering order, thanks to Jolene's bright idea to hit up old clients. Exhausted but dutiful, Jolene threw herself into action, and was 'not to be disturbed' for the rest of the night.

Twelve

Argus had snuck into the house and gone directly into his room, as quiet as a mouse. He was hungry and the bag of peanuts he'd brought with him didn't go very far, but he kept himself from leaving the room and wandering down to the kitchen, which is what his mind was doing every few minutes. In the meantime, he tried to concentrate on the small pile of newspaper articles beside him on the bed. There was a light tapping on the door, followed by Seth's head poking in, and his friendly voice that said,

"Hey man, what's shakin?", and Argus felt tremendously relieved and happy.

"Hey, come on on", he invited.

Seth popped in, closing the door swiftly and dramatically behind him, then took two giant steps to the little chair by the table. He swung it around and sat facing its back, with his arms on the top and his chin on his arms.

"So what's going on?" Argus asked.

"We didn't even know you were home. Been here awhile?"

"Couple of hours, I guess", Argus said. He felt a great need to explain himself, but didn't know where to begin. He couldn't think of anything else to say but waited for Seth to say something.

"Been reading those clippings again?" Seth inquired, pointing at the articles.

"Oh yeah", Argus said, happy to turn to something he could talk about. "There's some really weird stuff in these stories, man, weird."

"Which ones?"

"Like the dead woman", Argus continued. "The old lady named Pak, lived alone in her house. Some bill collector guy broke into her house and found her lying there dead on the floor. Been dead for days, they said later. And the doors and windows were all boarded up. Nailed shut good and tight. She left notes lying around. Said she was being hassled by ghosts.

Dead people coming up to the door, asking for help. Said they were lost. Freaking her out."

"Oh yeah, I remember now", said Seth. "Probably there were all just bill collectors like the guy who found her! And didn't she paint red circles all over the ceilings and walls?"

"Old lady went crazy", Argus decided. "I'm sure that happens a lot. Don't know why it's in with this package."

"It sure is a hodge podge", Seth said.

"But it's kind of like this other one too", Argus said. "The man who built a secret room in his house, and kidnapped his wife and locked her up in it. He said that he did it to keep her from vanishing. That was his word, said the cops. They were pretty sure he meant she kept running off, but he claimed that he meant the word literally. And his wife, she refused to testify against him. She said she was sure that he meant well."

"Odd couple", Seth said.

"Seven years", Argus told him. "He kept her locked up seven

years! Fed her okay, she was healthy and all. Spent quality time with his prisoner", he said.

"And she had a TV", Seth joked, cracking up.

"What more could you want?" Argus added.

"But seriously", Seth said upon recovering, "I mean really. What's up with these stories? And these photos and all of that stuff?"

"I got no idea", Argus said.

"We thought we had something today", Seth began, and he told him about the park and the map and the buildings and the bus route, and was adding that he now thought it was all a mistake, when Argus suddenly stopped him.

"The 63?" he asked.

"Yeah, the Venezia line", Seth replied. "Does that mean something to you?"

"My uncle was a bus driver", Argus told him. "And he drove that route, right up to the day that he vanished."

"Vanished?" Seth was surprised. "Do you mean that word literally like the guy in the paper?"

"Yeah", Argus brightened. "Literally. At least that's what everyone said. One day Uncle Charlie just vanished. He got off the bus at the end of the line, walked into a vacant lot and vanished. The passengers were sitting there patiently. Nobody saw where he went. After awhile somebody called up the Metro Authority and reported an AWOL driver. We never saw him again."

"How old were you? Do you remember the guy?"

"No", Argus said, "I must have been small, maybe four, maybe three, I don't know. I don't remember ever knowing him. My brother Alex does. He said they were friends. But nobody talked about Charlie, not in my house."

"Why not? Was he trouble?"

"No", Argus said, "I don't know. It's my family. Nobody ever talked about anything. It was pretty fucked up back there. A gathering of strangers. That's what I used to call 'dinner'", He tried to laugh, as if what he had said was amusing, but even Seth could tell it was painful.

"It's weird", he said. "Vanished. And the 63 line. Man, every time I think that there's nothing at all, there's something that ties into you. It's all about you, Argus. There's something there."

"Beats the hell out of me", Argus said, and the two men were quiet for awhile. Finally it was Seth who spoke up.

"You know what I think?" he said, and continued, "tomorrow is Saturday. You don't have to work, do you?" Argus shook his head.

"Me neither", he said. "We should go for a ride. I mean, Jolie and I drove all up and down, following that bus route, but that was driving. It's different. I was on the bus when I noticed those buildings. Driving I didn't see nothing at all. We should go on that bus. That's what I'm thinking."

Argus just shrugged. If he had to say what he really thought, he would say that it sounded like a complete waste of time, but he certainly had nothing better to do, and it could even be fun, to hang out with this guy, and do something different. As for the mystery, he really didn't know, and he really didn't care.

Thirteen

Seth was up bright and early Saturday morning, and made sure that Argus was too, although they hadn't actually agreed on a time to get going. Jolene knew all about their plan and was only sorry she was too busy to join them, but she wasn't too busy to fix them a large and healthy breakfast.

Seth knew, somehow, that the 63 didn't run very often on weekends but they could catch it near the half hour at Visitation and Hopland. They drove there and parked in an alley behind a barber shop. Argus didn't say much on the way. He was just following along, letting Seth do all the talking. Which he did. He talked about gardening. He talked about tools. He talked about machinery and chains and office supplies.

Argus had't realized what a chatterbox the guy was. He kept thinking, how'd he get to be like that? How's he find so much to say? Argus couldn't even think of a topic. He was trying, but nothing came to mind. Walking out to the nearly deserted boulevard, Seth suggested they should just wait and see which direction the first bus came, and then take that one. It wouldn't matter much, since the plan was to cover the whole route in each direction, hopping off whenever they saw something that might be interesting, and getting back on again with an all-day pass.

"I'll wait over there, and you wait here, and whichever one comes, the other one runs across," Seth proposed, and crossed the street. The two stood on opposite sidewalks looking up and down the street, while Seth occasionally did something goofy like hide behind a trash can and poke his head out when he spied Argus' startled expression, and call out, "hey man, over here", like a small child.

Argus was beginning to wonder what he'd gotten himself into. Usually on a Saturday he'd go off for a long walk somewhere, sit in a park and read some grim detective story. He'd been reading the Inspector Mole series, and had already plowed through thirty seven of the fifty eight books in the series. Part of him was already wishing he was doing that instead of whatever it was he actually was doing. Seth at least was enjoying himself, funning around, trying out silly walks and poses and basically showing off for anyone who might be looking. At last a bus arrived, a southbound bus headed down to the harbor. Seth dashed across in plenty of time to board along with Argus. Following, as usual, Argus sat where Seth had picked out seats, in the middle of the very back row.

"This way we can catch both sides", he proudly announced. There were only a few people on the bus, a couple of older women and the driver, a large and friendly fellow. The bus rolled off and halted every couple of blocks whether there were people waiting at the stop or not. The driver called out every intersection with equal flair.

"Cortland", he'd boom. "Next stop, Cortland Avenue".

Seth actively peered out the windows on both side, swiveling his head back and forth and still talking practically without interruption.

"My guess is we just might see that office park, or else the playground with the seesaw. Look, I brought my copies of the photos and the articles. Did you bring the originals? No? Just as well. I've got mine here. Want to look through them? Old lady in a black dress. Did you see an old lady in a black dress? Maybe one of the gals up front there? No? Well, she's supposed to be in a garden anyway. But if you see anything, just holler. Pull the rope, we'll get right off", but for all of his observing, neither of them saw anything of interest.

Argus wasn't really paying attention. He heard Seth's voice going in and out of his head, and the houses and buildings and cars they passed by barely registered either. The whole thing was a puzzle whose pieces didn't fit together. That was what he'd decided, and he wasn't going to try to figure it out. In just a few days he'd be twenty three years old, and nothing would happen, and nothing would change, and there was no good reason why anything should.

The bus turned off the boulevard and headed down some fairly small side streets, this way and that in a roundabout pattern that didn't yield any more passengers. Finally it came to the end in a rundown Old Town neighborhood close to the waterfront. The two old ladies got off at the very last stop, while Argus and Seth didn't move from their seats.

"This is it, boys", the bus driver called. "End of the line. We ain't going nowhere for another ten minutes"

"That's okay", Seth called back, "we're in no hurry."

"All right by me", said the driver, as he pulled out a cup that may have held coffee and glued it to his face for awhile.

"Excuse me", Seth said, after a couple of minutes, "How do you turn this thing around? Do you just back it up?"

"Oh no", said the driver, "We go through that little passage there", and he pointed to a gravelly alley that didn't seem wide enough for a bus to squeeze into, but it did, a few minutes later, when they took off again. They squished through the space between crummy apartment buildings close on either side, and past an opening between two of those that yielded a quick view of another side street, one that went directly to the waterfront.

"Holy shit", Seth jumped up, and pulled on the rope. "We've got to get off, man."

"What's up?" Argus asked. He had almost fallen asleep.

"Next stop's in two blocks", the bus driver called, as he

lurched the bus out of the side street onto a road.

"Come on", Seth grabbed Argus by the arm and pulled him up out of his seat. "We've got to go back there".

"Okay, okay", Argus said, shaking loose. He didn't like to be touched, and his irritation prevented him from even wondering what Seth was so damned excited about. He found out a few minutes later as they trudged up the sidewalk to the alley.

"It's the two red cars", Seth explained. "They're there, I saw them, at the end of the block".

"What red cars?" Argus asked.

"The ones in the photo", he said.

"At the office park?" Argus remembered.

"Yeah, but they're not. Look, look, there they are", and as they got closer he saw them. Two identical Audi three hundreds, fire engine red, parked squarely in front of a rundown, seemingly abandoned old bungalow, which was surrounded by a six foot high cyclone fence.

"It's the house!" Seth declared.

"The one with the family", Argus added.

"Yeah, but no family", said Seth. It was an incongruous sight. The cars looked shiny, brand new, and had customized license plates that read "HAUDI2" and "HAUDI3", but the bungalow was in very bad shape. Its white paint was peeling all over, and the windows were all boarded up with plywood adorned with spray painted tags. The driveway was shattered cement mostly covered by weeds.

"What are they doing here?" Seth wondered aloud, looking around for a sign of the drivers.

"Maybe they're out on the water", Argus suggested, and it was a reasonable idea. The harbor was only a few blocks away, and this was a discreet parking spot.

"Too inconvenient", Seth told him. "An Audi owner would never park here unless he had business."

"Could be trouble", Argus said, and Seth nodded. Seth was thinking of going on inside of the fence, since there was a gap in the corner that could easily be breeched, but Argus' comment made him think twice. Could be a drug deal, he thought. You don't want to get into that. So instead, he contented himself with walking around as much as he could.

A thick hedge covered one side of the yard, and behind it a drop to the water some ten feet below. Argus had trailed behind him that far, but they both turned around and went back to the cars. There, on the other side of the street, was a dusty old playground, filled with rusting swings and ancient equipment, including an old metal seesaw where two children were playing. Seth stared at Argus and said,

"I'm certain those kids were not there a minute ago".

"I don't know", Argus muttered, and he couldn't have said what he thought. He knew he had not noticed them, or even the park itself, but did that mean they weren't there? He felt like he was walking in fog, though the morning was sunny and clear. Seth crossed the street and, shuffling through his collection of papers, said

"They must be the boys in the photo".
"I don't think so", said Argus.

"One is a girl", and she was, though she could have easily passed as a boy.

She was taller and bigger than the other, and her hair was shorter, but she wore a similar outfit of denim and sneakers and tee. She was shouting as she pushed off the ground and soared up to the heights, while the boy seemed to hold on as best as he could. She was the one clearly driving that train. The children seemed very familiar to Argus. From ten feet away he was struck by how similar they were to his brother and his brother's friend Sapphire, when Alex and she were both around ten.

He kept drifting closer, but cautiously, as if they were wild creatures and he didn't want to scare them off. Seth was bolder, however, and walked straight up to the pair. The girl saw him coming and leaped off the seesaw, sending the boy crashing down on his butt. She was laughing as she shouted, running away,

"I'm going to the monkey bars. Last one there's a rotten egg!", as the boy picked himself off the ground, and hobbled after her.

"So like her", Argus said, and Seth turned to him and asked,

"Who?"

"What?" Argus stopped. "Oh, a kid I once knew. Of course it's not her. She's in Africa now, or somewhere like that. War correspondent, last thing I heard."

"Wow", Seth replied, impressed. When they looked back, the children were gone. Not on the monkey bars. Not in the playground. Just gone. The cars were still there, though, behind them, and the broken down house was there too. Argus shrugged.

"What do we do now?" he asked.

"Catch the next bus", Seth replied. They had hoped to see

more, to see something else, but that was their haul for the day. They saw a lot of the city, for sure. All the way across and all the way back, and the whole trip took more than five hours, including a lunch break and a coffee break, and a walk at the other far end. There they remembered the old football stadium, and how they'd both been there - Seth with his dad and Argus with Alex - to catch a Sea Dragons game now and then. The stadium had lasted less than ten years. It was beautiful, though, they agreed.

The Sea Dragons team moved to Nebraska, but still kept the name, which was weird. Joey Dalton, number ten, it turned out, was both of the guys' favorite player. That point of datum gave Seth enough ammo to chatter for another half hour. But the site of the stadium was a huge empty lot, nothing but rubble, and nobody was there except an old man at the very far end, who seemed to be dragging around some kind of metal detector.

"Good luck to that guy", was all Seth could say about that. Argus just grunted. He grunted a lot.

The truth of it was, he had nothing to say. The weird scene with the kids gave him something to think about, vague recollections of childhood, but the rest of the day he was dull. Seth kept trying his best to amuse, and Argus for his part tried as well, but by the end of the trip they were tired and gave up.

Argus felt bad, like he had nothing to offer. Anyone else would be more fun to hang out with than me, he reflected. Seth was just disappointed that they hadn't come up with more answers. Both were grateful to get back to the car and get home. Argus was hoping for a little alone time, but it seemed that was not in the cards.

Fourteen

Someone had left Todd and Brian alone, and if you did that, there was usually trouble. That was why Maribel always had plans. She had them both scheduled down to a tee; even their beer bouts were on her to-do list. As a professional planner, she had her boyfriend and his best friend arranged for convenience, usually hers, but they were happy enough. If she wanted to go to the movies, they did. If she wanted to go out to dinner, they did. When she wanted a ferryboat ride, they obliged. When she needed her evening, off to the pub they would dutifully go. Neither understood they were under her thumb. Both of them thought they were living their lives, but Maribel was running the show.

She knew from experience that their idle small minds were the devil's own playhouse. Sometimes, however, she slipped. That Saturday she and Jolene were too busy, the order they had was too big and complex. Often she'd dispatch the boys out on tasks, shopping or deliveries when no risk was involved, but this time it was just too important. She had to let them out of her sight. At first they rambled around in the yard, digging holes for no reason, looking for bones that some dog might have buried some time, if a dog ever lived at that house. There could be a box buried out in the yard holding masses of treasure, you just never knew. After making a mess out of that, they returned to the house but no games were on yet. It was Brian who had the idea to raid Argus' room.

"Come on", he goaded his buddy, "let's check this guy out. I mean, what do we really know about him?"

"Right on", said his pal, "let's go do it", so they charged to the front of the house (sliding in socks on the long wooden hallway floor, seeing who could slide best and the farthest) and tumbled into his bedroom. After poking around for a bit they found nothing; a bunch of small paperback books on the floor, dirty clothes, a clock and a lamp on the nightstand. Todd was already getting ready to leave when Brian called out,

"Hey dude, check it out", and held out the mystery package.

"What's up with that?" Todd wanted to know.

"I don't know, I just found it, under the bed".

"Under the bed, eh? Is it porn?" Todd was hoping it was. Brian dumped the contents onto the bed, and rummaging through them gave a low whistle.

"Some crazy shit", he declared. Todd picked up a couple of items, glanced at them briefly, and let them fall back.

"It's not porn", he concluded dejectedly.

"Fucking A", Brian agreed. "But cool. check it out. Couple box tops!"

"Big whoop", Todd retorted. "Come on, man, let's scoot. There's nothing in here."

"No wait", Brian said, "I got one of these. Sure I do".

"One of what?" Todd replied.

"A secret decoder ring", Brian said. "I didn't know they still made them. I've had mine since forever, since like when I was nine. It looks like exactly the same"

"What's it for?"

"Duh, secret codes", Brian said, "like this note". He picked up the handwritten scrawl.

"Got to be", he decided. "Bunch of words strung together, made for the ring. Hang on, I'll go get it", and he was gone in a flash. Todd went and stood by the window so that he could stand guard in case Argus came back unexpected. He didn't know where Argus had gone, or when he'd return. Someone ought to look out, he decided. Brian came back with the ring and sat down on the bed, with the note in one hand and the ring in the other. He'd also brought with him a pen and some paper. He went through the words one by one; and as he went through them a sentence emerged from the jumble of nonsense like 'elevator', 'storage', 'eleven', and 'lorakeet'.

"Got anything?" Todd kept on asking.

"It's coming, it's coming", Brian waved his friend off. "'Last house last stop'", sure it is, and then this, 'Final hour final day'. You see it goes like this. The first letter of the first word, then the second letter of the second word, and keep going like that until it starts over and then the same thing. And you pass each letter through the ring, you see? There it is"

"But what does it mean?" Todd wanted to know.

"Beats the hell out of me", Brian said. "But look at this shit. Huh". Todd was about to pester him with another dumb question when suddenly the front door opened, and Argus and Seth arrived home.

"Oh shit", Todd said. "Now we're fucked"

"Whatever", said Brian, unfazed. As Argus came into the room, Brian acted as if nothing was out of the ordinary.

"I decoded your note", he told Argus.

"You what?" Argus was too stunned to get it. The fact of those guys in his room with his stuff was a shock. He'd been trying to stay out of their way, having decided they had nothing to offer.

"Yeah, this note", Brian repeated, holding it up, and then

showing his paper to Argus. It was Seth, though, who snatched it and read it aloud.

"Last house last stop. Final hour final day. Man, that's awesome. How did you do it?" Brian explained about the secret decoder and Seth was struck dumb for a change. Todd, meanwhile, snuck out of the room and hightailed it back to his own, where he hid, waiting for Brian to give the all clear. Brian, though, was intrigued. Argus stood listening while Brian and Seth discussed the whole matter in detail.

"We know where the house is", Seth told him. "And we know what the day is. His birthday. And now we also know what time. Mystery solved!"

"I don't know about that", Argus said. "There's still a lot of loose ends, aren't there?"

"Let's go through it", Seth said, and they went through the items, one at a time. A lot of them could be crossed off as explained, but a lot of them still were unknown. The old lady in the garden, for one thing. The toy robots, another. And what about the house key? Seth couldn't answer the first two, but the key had to be to the house, he was sure. And the politician? Brian could answer that one.

Turned out the frat boy had a thing for the news. "That was an excellent story", he told them. "There's this guy, see, Daniel Fulsom. Actually he's in a few of these stories, now that I'm looking at them. Remember he owned the Sea Dragons? Well, that was after he got out of jail. He was a bankster, see? Had his own financial mafia going on. One time he owned the whole city council, got them to give him these contracts. All the garbage, the trucking, construction, if it was city money he was getting it. Cheap bastard too. Billionaire but he did shoddy work. Then one of his buildings came tumbling down. Crappy materials, that was the word, but not according to him. He came out with this story that there is this monster, you see, no really, a monster, that ate out the concrete foundation. Took it all out. I forget now exactly his story."

"Anybody ever see this monster?" Seth wanted to know.

"Course not", said Brian, "and anyway, he shut up pretty quick. I just remember I heard it somewhere. It wasn't all over the place. Oh yeah, there's this book, the one in this article here.

'The Witchcraft of Positive Thinking'. Fulsom was all into that. He figured he'd paid his dues with his prison time, but then maybe he didn't, maybe he owed, more than he thought."

"I don't know what you are talking about", Argus said. "I thought that was some kind of self help book"

"Yeah, yeah", Brian said, "it is. It's got this idea that you can get what you want, but only if you're willing to pay the price, and so of course the more you want, the more it costs. Fulsom, you see, he wanted a lot. It costs if you want to have billions. Well, that's the idea, I guess."

"How can you pay for money?" Seth was puzzled, "that just doesn't make any sense."

"You don't only pay in one way", Brian explained, "like I said about jail. He thought that would pay for his wishes. Turned out that he had to pay more. Loss. He paid a lot in loss, like when Fulsom Towers went down. Seventeen people were killed in that crash. Lucky for him it was night and mostly night watchmen and cleaners in there. Even so, he got sued, by the city and families and unions and everyone. Cost him a bundle, and then there was Sea Dragons stadium."

"What about that?" Seth asked, "I always heard it was damaged."

"Nothing was wrong with the place", Brian told them. "Only thing wrong was Dan Fulsom's head. He came to think he was cursed. Rumors were going the stadium was haunted. Strange shit was happening there. Unexplained and unexplainable. Didn't you ever hear about that?"

Argus and Seth shook their heads.

"I guess most people don't know", Brian said. "A friend of mine worked for him once. Told me I shouldn't tell anyone, so don't say you heard it from me. Well, old Fulsom took to hiding out. Hardly anyone's seen him in years. He's got agents who run things for him, and the agents go around hiring folks to do the strangest things. Like my friend. He says one time they paid him just to go and stand in line for an hour. People say he's gone crazy, batshit insane. Talks to the walls. Seeing things. This monster, you see, it lives under the city, and it comes out sometimes and it does crazy things."

"Like what?" Argus asked

"Crazy things", Brian repeated himself. "According to Fulsom, of course. My friend never saw anything. Anyway, Fulsom sold the football team and tore down the place for no reason. Fucking Nebraska Sea Dragons! What a joke. And ever since then, he has stayed out of sight"

"We've been seeing some crazy stuff too", Seth said. He told Brian about the old men in the park that Jolene saw, and the kids on the seesaw they just saw, and related what old Captain Havenaard told him too.

"It seems like it could be all normal taken one at a time", he concluded, "all of those things don't seem strange necessarily. It's only with all of this stuff together and now, and all of it pointing at him", meaning Argus, who was still standing in his own room like an intruding guest.

"Don't look at me", Argus said, "I don't know anything about anything."

"Well, it's your birthday on Tuesday", Seth told him. "I've got a feeling that it's going to be one to remember. Man, this is so exciting"

"Yeah it's pretty cool", Brian agreed. Argus didn't feel the same way. He was just wishing that they would just get the hell out of his room.

Fifteen

Argus didn't get his wish until much later. In the meantime, Jolene found out about the secret decoding and had to be filled in on the day's adventure as well, and Maribel wandered up from the kitchen, not wanting to be left out, and even Todd emerged from hiding as well when he figured out it was safe. Jolene was ecstatic that everything was figured out, and decided that on Tuesday night they'd have a big birthday party for Argus and then everyone would venture out together on an expedition to the chosen site at the chosen time.

Argus didn't want a party, or any more adventures, really, but what could he say? Everyone else wanted to have a good time, so why should he be a spoilsport? He'd just go along if it made them all happy. All six were crowded into Argus' room and it was just too much for him, so he was the one who had to leave. During a moment when they were all jabbering at once, he made his way out the door and out of the house entirely. By the time he'd walked around the block a few times he could see that they'd finally vacated his room and he snuck back in, and didn't come out again that night.

Very early the next morning he left again and spent the entire day Sunday alone in the big park down the street, with some stale rolls, out of season oranges and the next Inspector Mole mystery. He wasn't quite sure why he read those books. The Inspector never seemed able to crack any case, yet somehow everything always worked out. Argus himself never bothered trying to figure out who did what or why. For one thing, he didn't care, and for another, the books were never written like that. They were genuine mystery novels, where the mystery often remained mysterious, unlike most books of that type, which should really be called "solution" novels, because there is rarely any mystery left by the end. Still, Argus absorbed the books and was determined to complete the entire series. It felt good to have the day to himself and by late afternoon almost felt like his regular self again. He was even almost looking forward to going back to work the next day, just to get back to routine.

"It is natural feeling", Mikael said to him, when he explained that very thought the next day. "People being animal creatures of this particular planet."

They were surrounded by a mountain of incoming boxes,

typical for a Monday morning, when the supplies replenishing the weekend sales poured in from delivery trucks from as early as four in the morning. Chattering made the work go faster, and Mikael was very good at doing the former, while Argus specialized in the other.

"This particular planet", Mikael continued to say, "is a rhythmic and cyclical planet. It rotates, and it revolves. It has one sun. It has one moon. It has the day and it has the night. Much of the planet has seasons too. The animal creatures that live on this planet have cycles as well. They sleep and they wake. They hunt and they eat. They have young and grow old. They live and they die."

"Isn't it probably like that on every planet with life?" Argus wanted to know, and Mikael merely shrugged and went on.

"Who can say? Who can know? We just know how it is on this one. Other planet may have two suns. There are systems like that. And many have several moons. Who can say what it means? Creatures on planets like that may turn red, may turn blue, may not sleep, merely change. But on this one the creatures have cycles. Air goes in, air goes out. Blood is pumped, blood returns. If the things that you do fit into a rhythm, then you feel good, it is right. It is why there is music. Why there is chanting. Meditation. Repetition. Hypnosis. All good if it makes you feel good."

"Religion", Argus added thoughtfully.

"The good part of that, yes for sure", Mikael said. "Not the politics part, the power trip part. The organized parts are of ritual, routine. Get you into the rhythm. All good"

"All good?" a voice came through from the swinging shop doors. It was Jolene, who had come down to pick up supplies for the party, and also to ask something of Argus.

"Hi", Argus said when he saw her, and Mikael said,

"Pretty lady, hello!"

Jolene smiled and walked into the storeroom.

"Jolene", she said, holding out her hand and taking Mikael's said, "you must be Mikael."

"I was thinking you must be Jolene", he replied, taking her hand gently and shaking it. "I have heard about you. But how have you heard about me?"

"We both solved the 600 day puzzle", she said and he smiled.

"I forgot. Argus told me. I thought I was first."

"Maybe you were", she replied, and turned to Argus and said,

"I wanted to ask if there was anyone else that you want to invite to the party. Maybe your brother?"

"Well", Argus said,

"I'm sure he is busy. I don't know. Mikael, if he wants to, I guess". How could he not say Mikael, he said to himself, when the guy was just standing there, acting all nice?

"What is this party?" Mikael wanted to know.

"For his birthday", Jolene explained. "Tomorrow night. Can

you come?"

"Is it tomorrow already? I forgot. The big day. The day that the sequence will end"

"Yes, and the final hour of the final day", Jolene said. "The last house at the last stop." Mikael studied her face to try and see if that was a joke. Jolene, seeing his confusion, explained about the secret decoded message. Argus hadn't bothered to tell him.

"Now I'm sure I will come", he announced. "I wonder, what could it be?"

"Is there anyone else?", Jolene asked Argus, and he shook his head 'no'.

"What about Madam Sylvia?" Mikael said, laughing. "After all, she has been part of the mystery too. She saw all the items and who knows, she could help."

"Oh come on", Argus said, getting annoyed.

"It was only a joke", Mikael said.

After an awkward few moments when no one had anything further to say, Jolene handed Mikael a nicely handwritten invitation to the party, with directions to their house, and the time. Jolene always did such things nicely. After saying goodbye, she went back to her shopping, and purchased everything that she needed. While she was carrying the bags to Seth's car, she happened to look up and notice Madam Sylvia's storefront on the other side of the street.

"Well, why not?" she said to herself.

She was hoping that Argus would have a few people he wanted to come. As it was, it was only the household, and now also Mikael. She put the stuff away in the trunk and went over to see Madam Sylvia. Sylvia was not surprised to see her. She was never surprised to see anyone. She figured it was another young lady who wanted to know if she would get married, have children and when. The first thing she said, though, was

"I can see you will be successful in business".

"I know that", Jolene answered right back.

"Oh?" Sylvia wondered, "how do you know?"

"Well, I'm good at what I do and I work very hard, and I never give up. That's how I know", Jolene told her. "But I didn't come see you for that", and she explained about Argus' party and for one Sylvia was completely off guard. The last thing she expected was a stranger to walk in and invite her to somebody's party.

"Thank you, that will be nice", she replied, as Jolene handed her one of her custom invites, and just as suddenly as she'd decided to come and had come, Jolene decided to go and was gone, not having told Sylvia anything, really. The fortune teller watched her depart, examined the note in her hand, realized it was slightly scented and sniffed it, said "nice", and went back inside.

Sixteen

The party of course was a good one. Maribel and Jolene, after all, did parties for a living. They had lots of delicious hors d'oeuvres, including a range of exotic olives, tasty Asian chicken wings, miniature crab cakes, and crackers and cheeses. While the women were preparing these things, they kept sending Todd around the living room with trays. He felt more like an employee than a guest, and it was weird to be serving his house mates. Brian in particular kept taunting him, making him wait while he decided which treat he desired, then calling him back and changing his mind. That little routine kept Seth cracking up. He never got tired of the joke.

Mikael had originally hung out with Argus, but Argus having nothing to say, and Mikael being something of a lady's man in his own mind at least, took to hovering around the passage to the kitchen, where he watched the young women at work. They shared a glance of agreement to ignore him, which he noticed, and did understand. He was the happiest one in the house, then, when Sylvia arrived. Although he had only mockingly suggested inviting her, he dashed up and welcomed her in, as if he were the gallant host. He even led her around, introducing her to all the others he didn't really know. He decided he would not leave her side, since she was the only game in town, so he didn't.

He stuck right with her while she also attempted and failed to make a conversation with Argus, and he stayed by her side while she bantered a little with Brian and Seth. Brian as usual said something rude. In this case it was,

"How do you get to be psychic anyway? Is there like a trade school or something for that?", and when Sylvia replied that no, that actually she'd simply been born with it, but she did have a Master's Degree in Astrophysics from the University of Leeds, Mikael saw his opening and went for it.

"That is quite a coincidence", he told her. "I myself went to Leicester"

"Really?" Sylvia finally took notice of him. "What did you major in there?"

"Well, actually", he said modestly, "I have a Ph D in Mathematics" Sylvia was not the only one startled. Argus had sort of been listening in, and piped up,

"What are you doing in shipping receiving?"

"I just like it", Mikael told everyone. "I did not want to teach, so what else can you do? I did research a bit. I was lonely. I had chances to be working at Oxford, also St. Petersburg. I thought no. I will go to America."

"What kind of research?" Sylvia wanted to know.

"Quantum numbers", he told her, and from then on he had won. Sylvia was fascinated with that area in particular, and soon they had left the others behind in complete and utter confusion. They drifted off to a corner to continue their chat, absorbed each other completely in science and were interrupted only by the occasional offerings of food, provided by Todd. At length Maribel and Jolene finished up in the kitchen, and came out and joined in the party.

Brian and Seth had stocked up on beer and were listing their favorite musicians, in both chronological and alphabetical order. Todd hurried to catch up and pounded some brews. Maribel followed her pattern of a bottle of wine leading to a revival of historical dancing routines. Jolene made sure that everyone had something to do. The trouble for her was Argus, who didn't drink anything ever but water, who didn't look happy, and who was standing alone by the door leading out to the back yard. She could sense he was eyeing escape, so she singled him out for attention. Most people gave up on Argus after trying to drum up a talk, and failing.

"You don't like to talk much, do you?" she asked him.

"I guess not", he said.

"Were you always this way?" she wanted to know. Argus nodded.

"But you seem to be always thinking a lot", she went on, and although Argus shook his head in disagreement, she said,

"What do you think about? That's what I want to know."

"Nothing much", Argus said. "I really don't think very much."

"What about tonight?" she asked. "What do you think's going to happen? It's going to be time pretty soon."

"I don't think anything will happen", he said. "I'm starting to think it was all a big hoax."

"But the clues", Jolene said, "they're all adding up. To what I don't know, but to something."

"Or to nothing", he said. He was wishing he could just be more positive. It was nice, having Jolene to himself, nice to be close to her, to see her looking at him, to be looking at her, into her beautiful green eyes. He wanted to seem grateful and happy, he wanted to make her think he appreciated what she was doing for him.

"It's a really nice party", he said.

"You don't mean it", she said back. "I can see, you don't really like parties, do you?"

"No", he admitted, thinking "that didn't work".

"Well, I'm sorry", she said, turning away, but she wasn't. Everyone else was having fun, and it was almost time to get going.

"Hey everybody!", she shouted, and shouted again to get their attention. "It's already ten thirty. We ought to be getting a move on" People started shuffling toward the front of the house when Maribel suddenly remembered the cake. In their hurry they forgot to light candles or sing. Instead, she just sliced up the thing and made Todd go around and hand everyone a plate. Seth was trying to organize cars and there was general confusion about where they were going and who would drive what and who would take who. Finally Sylvia announced, and Mikael took up the call, that she had a large VW Eurovan, and everyone could go with her in that. It was decided. They all pushed outside and piled in, with Argus and Brian and Seth in the back, Maribel and Todd and Jolene in the middle, Mikael in the front and Sylvia driving.

Seventeen

Sylvia knew the way so she safely ignored Seth's shouted directions, which she really couldn't hear well anyway. She had spent many hours as a child along the harbor, helping her dad with the rigging of his sailboat. Her father had been a sailor who was often at sea, but whenever he was home he spent most of his time as close to the water as possible. He had been dead for many years now, and Sylvia felt a bit sad as she drove by their old familiar haunts. Her passengers, of course, were oblivious to that, and to most everything else as well. Many of them were pretty well drunk, and the ones that were not were thinking about the mission at hand. As they got closer they began once again talking about the adventure.

Every one seemed to have a different idea of what could possibly happen. Seth simply thought there'd be a package by the fence, a birthday present from Argus' brother. Brian concluded there'd be a big sign with a face with its tongue sticking out, saying 'nyaah nyaah nyahh'. Todd thought there'd be Treasure Hunt Two, with another small package with more random clues. Maribel assumed it was cake. Jolene figured that the person responsible would be waiting there, shouting

'SURPRISE!', and that it was someone from Argus' past. Mikael didn't make a suggestion, but privately he was agreeing with Todd. Only Argus thought there'd nothing. Nothing and no one, nothing at all, and that soon they'd be back in the car, heading home, and everything would finally go back to normal.

Normal was the last thing they saw as the car turned and entered the block. The previous streets had been empty, no people, no traffic, which wasn't surprising. It was a weeknight, nearly eleven o'clock, and it was a sparsely populated and strictly residential neighborhood. On the last street, however, there were people, maybe a dozen or more, in groupings of one or two or three at most. They were all walking, slowly, right down the middle of the road, towards the end of the block.

Sylvia slowed the car down to a crawl and came up behind them. None of the people moved out of the way. Mikael whistled, softly.

"This doesn't look right", he whispered, as the passengers quieted into a hush. The people on the street staggered forward, steadily onward, each in silence, intent on their final destination.

"I think I'll park here", Sylvia said, and she did. They were still several houses away from the end.

"The cars aren't there", Seth announced and when people looked back at him questioningly he added, "the Audis. The red ones. Those cars aren't there".

He was right. There were no cars at all on the block except Sylvia's. All of the houses were dark and the few streetlights on were quite dim. Mikael opened his door and stepped out. He turned and pulled open the sliding middle door, and starting with Jolene, all the passengers began to emerge. Only Todd in the back didn't move.

"Um, I think I'll stay here", he quietly said.

"Me too", said Maribel, as she jumped back into the car.

"That's a good idea", Sylvia said. "You two should really spend a little more time together, alone, if you're even considering marriage some day".

Todd and Maribel looked at each other and shrugged. Then Maribel reached over and closed the side door. Brian and Seth were already joining the line, though by this time the others were well down the road. Argus and Jolene followed behind, with Sylvia and Mikael behind them. It was a very odd looking procession. The ones in the front were dirty and ragged. Most of them looked like they'd never been washed. Their clothes were smelly and torn. Most were old men, unshaven and stumbling. A couple were women, with twisted up faces and clothes that didn't quite fit. One was a young man, the last in the line, with wide open eyes as if startled.

In silence they arrived at the house, the last house, and squeezed through the gap in the tall cyclone fence. They walked up to the door and went in.

"Fucking spooky", said Brian, and Seth only nodded. They were the first to arrive of the group, and they waited for the others to join them.

"There's no lights on in there", Brian added.

"No sounds coming out of there either", said Seth.

"What's the story?" Jolene asked, coming up to meet them. Brian and Seth shook their heads.

"I don't know". When Mikael and Sylvia arrived they all stood and stared at the house, which remained as silent and dark as the rest on the street.

"There's no packages waiting out front", Seth noted.

"Think we ought to go in?" Jolene asked.

"Well, we did come this far", Brian said, but nobody moved.

"What do you think?" Mikael asked Sylvia, and she thought for a minute, then said,

"We might as well see what there is", so it was decided.

Brian went through the gap in the fence first, and when the whole group got to the steps, and Brian went up to the door, he looked back and asked,

"Wasn't there a key in that package?"

"Oh shit", said Seth. "Did you bring the key?" he asked Argus.

"Sorry", said Argus. "I didn't even think of it"

"Fuck", Brian said. "Well that's that", and he really felt very relieved. He started to move down the step when Mikael spoke up and said,

"Maybe the door is not locked. I didn't see any of the other people knock or use a key." Brian turned back and tried the door knob. Creaking, the door swung wide open. Brian hesitated, so Seth brushed right past him and he went in first. He tried the light switches. They didn't work.

"I'll bet nobody brought a damn flashlight, either", he said, but then there was light. It was Sylvia.

"I thought to bring mine out from the car", she said as she handed it to Seth, who was leading the way.

"Okay, thanks", he said, then took a deep breath. "No more

excuses, people. Let's move out, and see what is what".

It was a small house. From the front entry way you could go right or left, into the sole bedroom on the right, or through the living room on the left, then on the kitchen, with a bathroom past that. There was no one inside besides them, and from the looks of it, no one had been there for a very long time. The dishes in the cupboards were grimy, but dry. No food was in evidence anywhere. The couch and the chair in the front room were dusty and covered in cobwebs. In the bedroom, a rusty box spring sat with no mattress, and there were no signs of residents other than mice, whose droppings were all over the floors.

"Where'd they all go?" Brian asked. "They were right there in front of us. We saw them go in. What the fuck?"

"Maybe they all went out back", Seth suggested, so Brian and Seth headed out through the back steps into a yard that was littered with stuff. Old stuff, broken stuff, metal, cloth, and wood. It looked like a long abandoned ship-building site.

Jolene had stayed back in the kitchen, where she inspected a very old stove, an antique that was quite to her liking. Mikael and Sylvia had retreated back out to the street, where they stood in the front yard and talked about math. Brian made his way through the clutter to the very back edge, which opened straight to a long drop down to the water with no fence or wall to keep you from falling right in. He peered over and thought he could see the remains of a pier, or at least pieces of timber sticking out of the water.

Seth, in the meantime, had found a storm door, an entry way into the crawlspace. 'At least I have the flashlight', he said to himself as he pried it open with a stray crowbar and let himself in.

Argus was left all alone in the bedroom. He just stood there, thinking 'I ought to do something'. He noticed a closet door next to the bed and went over and opened it. Nothing inside. 'No surprise', he said to himself. He took a step inside and peered around in the darkness, and felt a strange sensation of dizziness, as if the world was suddenly spinning faster.

Eighteen

He turned around to find himself not in the bedroom, but in a different and unfamiliar room. It was maybe seven by nine, dimly lit by a night light plugged into the wall, but no windows or furniture except for one rickety old wooden chair in the middle, and a shelf on the wall holding two tiny objects. He walked over to them, picked them both up, held them up to his face, and in the dim light he realized that they were a pair of toy robots, identical to the ones in the mystery package. While examining them, he felt a chill breeze and shivering, turned around to see a man standing behind him.

"You don't know me", the man said, "but I know you. I'm Dan Fulsom, and you're Argus Kirkham. You are the price that I have to pay."

Argus gasped and blinked several times to make sure he was not seeing things. Fulsom was a short, sweaty man with foolish sideburns, wearing an unhappy brown suit and matching fedora. He seemed quite at ease in the room and began to pace back and forth.

"It's the dragon, you know. It demands to be fed. But not just any old body will do. I've been trying to feed it for years. I've given it old people, sick people, homeless, unwanted. Criminals, thugs and old whores. It takes them all in but it spits them back out. Every one of them comes back to haunt me, like a boomerang". He spat out these last words with anger. Facing Argus again he went on.

"I must have a sacrifice, one that will stick and stay put, that the dragon will take, and keep. The ghosts have told me who it wants. It wants the one that got away."

"I have no idea what you are talking about", Argus finally spoke up. And really he thought, 'this guy is just nuts' and he remembered what Brian had told him, that nobody ever sees this guy, that he's hold up in secret somewhere, and Argus was astonished to realized that this was the place, the secret room, the place where the crazy man lives.

"You say that you don't", Fulsom said, "but you do. Maybe you've simply forgotten. You were only a child at the time, a small child. It was you who could see it, you who it wanted. You didn't go in. You let Uncle Charlie go first, but it didn't want him. It kept spitting him out. It was you that it wanted. You that it wants"

"What it?" Argus asked, "what's this thing you keep talking about?"

"The dragon. I told you. It lives down below. It lies under the city and waits. When it sees what it wants, it comes up. It has powers. It can look like whatever it wants, whatever will suit its convenience. It attracts like a flower and kills like a snake. For you, it looked like a bus. It wanted to take you away, and you almost did. Then the girl came and snatched you away, right when you were about to get on board"

"Oh", Argus said, finally remembering. "You mean Sapphire. You don't really believe in that story, do you? That was all just make believe. They told me about that when I was a kid, to explain what happened to my uncle. It's like Santa Claus, or the Easter Bunny. They called it Snapdragon Alley, but you know and I know that's just the name of the mall you built, over by Sea Dragons stadium."

"It was true", Fulsom told him. "Not just a story. It really did happen, you know".

"No way", Argus said. "It's a family joke."

"It's no joke", Fulsom told him, beginning to lose patience. "It is real. You've seen it yourself. You've just seen the ghosts. You must know by now . Your friends all believe. They know that it's true."

"My friends only want to believe", Argus said. "They want to have fun. They took some everyday ordinary coincidences and made a big pattern of it. We always see things when we want to believe in them. Old men playing cards in the park. Kids on a seesaw. Red cars, parked on the street. You can see those thing every day if you want to and if you look hard enough and long enough and in enough places."

"You just saw the ghosts a few minutes ago", Fulsom insisted. "There's no use denying or pretending".

"I did see some people out on the street. They were probably going to some party somewhere. I don't know where they got to, but I really don't care. There's no monster", Argus said.

"There's no curse. There's just you. I heard you went crazy. Everybody says so. I guess all your money didn't help you with that."

"I know what I know", Fulsom said, "and you know it too. You've belonged to the dragon ever since that one day. Haven't you noticed? Your whole life, since then, you've been half in the world and half out. You don't even know who you are, you don't even know what you want. You go around like a zombie and that's what you are, a kind of a zombie. It reached out and touched you. It had you and lost you. That girl, that Sapphire, the one who pulled you away, you don't know what she did. She thought she had saved you, but really she killed you. She should have let you go in. If only she had let you go in"

"I'm going out now", Argus said, but looking around, he noticed there wasn't a door he could see.

"You're not going anywhere", Fulsom declared, and Argus noticed that Fulsom was holding a gun in his hand.

"I don't like to be so crude", Fulsom said." Usually I use more civilized means, but this time, I can't afford to do that"

Fulsom raised the gun and pointed it straight at Argus, who discovered that somehow he couldn't seem to move. It was as if he'd grown roots and was tied to the spot. He felt something pulling, like a weight pulling down on his feet from below and then suddenly he heard a bang and went crashing down through the floor. 'I must have banged my head on something', he thought, and then he felt someone tug on his arm and heard a familiar voice that said "Hey man, what's shakin?"

Nineteen

"Holy shit", Argus said, "what the fuck?"

"I think we had better skedaddle", Seth told him, as he scrambled to his feet and ducking, headed back out to the door leading out to the yard, Argus following behind them.

"Hurry up", Seth called out, "I think he's behind you".

Fulsom had also come down through the hole. Seth had been down there the whole time, listening, and it was just dumb lock that Argus was standing on a heating vent and that the floor was so old and so rotten that Seth was able to pull it down with only a crowbar he'd found in the yard and brought along just in case. Argus and Seth crawled as fast as they could on their hands and their knees, coming into the yard all out of breath.

"Hey guys", Brian said as he saw them emerge. "Anything interesting down there?"

"Guy's got a gun", Seth managed to say as he leaped and

rolled over some old boards for cover, Argus copying his every move.

"A what?" Brian asked him, confused. Fulsom came out shooting wildly and missing.

"Oh fuck", Brian said, and looking around, picked up a piece of old rebar and brought the thing down as hard as he could on the gun, knocking it out of Fulsom's hand. The gun clattered among some driftwood and vanished from sight.

At the sounds of the shots, Mikael had come running, and piled on as Brian had jumped onto Fulsom. They soon had him pinned and though Fulsom struggled, Mikael got his arm in a very tight grip, and threatened to pull it right out its socket. Jolene, right above them, opened the window, and did as Seth said and called the nine one one on her cellphone.

Argus and Seth got to their feet. Argus was still in shock. He kept shaking his head and repeating to himself, over and over again, "Son of a bitch. It was just a trap the whole time!"

Seth was bleeding. He'd managed to scratch himself on old

wooden nails several places. Sylvia had followed Mikael to the back and, once again congratulating herself on her foresight, pulled out the first aid kit she'd brought from the car along with her flashlight. She was cleaning and bandaging Seth when they first heard the sirens.

"You're a handy one to have around", Mikael told her while tightening his hold. "But you probably knew I was going to say that"

"You could try and surprise me sometime", she replied, and gave him a warm little smile.

Fulsom kept trying to talk, although Brian kept pushing his face in the dirt.

"Shut the fuck up", Brian said. "I don't like people shooting my friends"

"It's going to get you", Fulsom was ranting, "maybe not this time, but some day it will."

"What the hell are you talking about?" Mikael asked. "No,

don't tell me. I don't want to know."

"It's his birthday", Jolene yelled in genuine outrage. "You're supposed to get PRESENTS when it's your birthday." She was always a stickler for tradition.

Argus just laughed, really laughed for the first time in years. He felt like a spell had been broken, like a price had been paid and a curse had been lifted, but that was what Fulsom was after, he reminded himself.

"All that for nothing", he shouted at Fulsom. "For nothing. You hear me? For nothing!"

"One day", Fulsom started to answer, but Mikael pulled back on his arm and he stopped.

"Forget it", said Argus, and he walked away. He made it as far as the front of the house, where he sat down on a crumbling cement step and looked up at the clear night sky as the sirens drew closer and closer.

1692198R0009

Printed in Great Britain
by Amazon.co.uk, Ltd.,
Marston Gate.